The Artemis Conspiracy

By Gerard Hansen

The Artemis Conspiracy
Copyright © 2014
Cheetahtech International L.L.C. Port St Lucie, FL
ISBN 978-0-9916067-3-3
Library of Congress Control
Number: 2015900644

COVER DESIGN BY JENNIFER HARRIS

Dedicated to all those who passionately seek the truth.

Acknowledgements

I am deeply grateful to Shirley Moore and Julie Hasenhuettl for their tireless work on research, editing, and formatting the manuscript. Jennifer Harris was the driving force designing the cover.

Preface

The Artemis Conspiracy is a dramatic story of financial greed, the lust for power and government corruption. In this dark environment, good people are heroically trying to solve difficult problems. A team of dedicated doctors and scientists battle a deadly epidemic. An aggressive newspaper reporter exposes the shady activities of powerful people, risking his life to get the story. The Director of National intelligence and her young protégé attempt to unravel a global conspiracy. They are all brought together in twists and turns of the plot.

This story is fiction, but is consistent with economic, political, and social trends. Names of individuals or groups are fictitious. Any resemblance to real people, living or deceased is coincidental.

Scientific fraud and misconduct are rare occurrences. The vast majority of scientists are honest. Scientific Truth is not determined by a majority vote, but by experiment and replication by peers. Scientists are collectively aware that their careers depend on their reputation for integrity. I have overemphasized science malfeasance, because even rare occurrences can have disastrous results.

One

Tyler stood knee-deep in the swirling Ogallala River as he gazed on the relief of the tall pines against the soft blue sky. This is Paradise, he thought, as the flowing water gently massaged his calf muscles. He cast the fly out to see if he could entice another trout. The finicky fish leapt from the water to grab a more attractive morsel. The competition was tough this week.

Suddenly, a hot flash swept over Tyler and his empty stomach spasmed. He stumbled out of the water and collapsed on the stone bank. As if on cue, a large black wolf leapt from the tree line and snapped its jaws onto his bicep. A red mist sprayed over Tyler's face, as the canine teeth ripped through flesh and blood vessels.

"Get it off! Get it off!" he screamed, thrashing about desperately. His cousins, Seth and Albert, came running up.

"What's wrong with him?" asked Albert.

"I think he's hallucinating!" Seth replied. Albert wheeled and ran back to the cabin to call for help.

Dust swirled in the wind as Rescue One raced down the dirt road. Two men sprang from the truck, and started to run down the bank. They cursed as they slipped and nearly fell on the shifting gravel.

"What happened?" shouted Scotty, the Senior EMT.

"He's half burning up and freakin out!" shouted Seth.

The firemen began to examine and immobilize him.

"He's hot as hell. My scope says one-o-six," Scotty observed. "You guys have any ice?"

"Only what's in the chests to chill the beer," Seth replied.

"We'll have to commandeer it and pack him in ice!" Scotty ordered.

Seth was astonished. "You don't have anything better?" he asked.

"Our chill blanket's broken, and our wise town fathers haven't given us any money to replace it," Scotty explained.

They realized they couldn't get Tyler up the steep embankment to the ambulance. Seth, Scotty, and Albert strapped Tyler to the board and cautiously walked along the stony riverbank. The driver struggled up the steep hill to back up the truck. A crow squawked loudly, as if mocking them for their efforts. They packed ice around their distraught patient and loaded him into the ambulance.

The driver gunned the engine and began to race down the dirt road, kicking up an enormous dust cloud. He clicked on the radio and began the protocol:

"Smoky Ridge, Smokey Ridge, Centerville One transporting male patient, age thirty-four. High fever, blood pressure and delirious. Sending vitals. ETA twenty minutes."

"Copy, Centerville One," the calm voice from the hospital said. "Do you have a line in yet?"

"Hell no!" shouted Scotty. "He's thrashing around too much! I'll mark the data feed when I get him fastened down and get the needle in!"

"Stay calm, Scott," counseled the driver.

"You want to switch places?" snapped Scotty. "This guy's got muscles like a gorilla!"

"We're only getting sporadic heart signals," nagged the disembodied voice from the hospital.

"Same problem here!" Scotty yelled. "He's ripping off the pads!"

*****

At Smoky Ridge Medical Center, Doctor Judy Peterson prepared her ER team. The body temp read-out caught her eye immediately. "Gowns, gloves, and masks!" she shouted. "Prepare Isolation 2."

Activity was fast but orderly. Everyone knew the drill all too well. It had only been a few years since the prion epidemics had come calling. They took the lives of two elderly hospital staff. Their pictures hung in the hallway as a memorial and a reminder.

The stretcher crashed through the swing doors of the ER and the team sprang into action.

"Get rid of this piece of crap and get me an accurate body temp!" Peterson demanded.

Scotty took offense. "We just calibrated that meter last week!" he retorted.

"I might have believed it if you hadn't brought me a patient packed in ice!" she quipped. "If you brought me a false crisis, Centerville is going to owe us for the isolation fee!"

A short, slightly built nurse settled the dispute. "One hundred five-point-five," she chirped.

Peterson nodded to Scotty. "You're right, and now you get to hang around for decontamination." Turning back to the team, she barked out the orders: "Stat AC-8 culture, blood panel, and quick-tox!"

After hours of cooling and balancing fluids, the ER team felt they were making little progress. The temp meter had only dropped to one-hundred-four.

"His skin is getting very red from contact with the blanket!" the circulating nurse warned.

Peterson looked frustrated, but her voice was calm. "We have to try to save his brain. We'll worry about the freezer burn later."

Results were beginning to post on the screen mounted on the wall of the isolation unit.

"Negative on the AC-8 cultures," shouted the young intern, who was monitoring the data. "Dengue fever is out too. Also negative on the quick-tox!"

Tyler began to struggle again. "It's the devil! Get him off! He's choking me!" he screamed.

A loud snap made everyone jump. "Dammit!" shouted Peterson. "He broke his forearm!"

An examination looked like both radius and ulna had snapped. "We're trying to save his brain, but we're going to need sedation," mused Peterson.

"Let's titrate him with Somnaxn and put a rigid cast on that arm. We don't want him slicing open an artery."

*****

Pam and Maureen, the two young nurses from the ER team, sat in the decontamination lounge. Their hair was wrapped in lemon-accented antibiotic towels. The sun was beginning to set behind the North Carolina Smoky Mountains. The wind outside produced a kaleidoscope of flickering shadows through the room.

Maureen was the first to break the silence. "That was really spooky. Do you really think he might be possessed by the devil?"

Pam wrinkled her nose in disapproval. "Don't let Judy hear you talking like that," she cautioned. "She's a straight-up science geek; I feel really bad though. He's really cute!"

"Yeah," Maureen agreed, "and his cousins are pretty hot too."

Five minutes later, as if they had been summoned, Albert and Seth strolled in.

"Hey," Albert said, "are you gals taking care of Tyler Chapman?"

The nurses both nodded as they self-consciously pulled the towels from their heads.

"So why are they keeping us in the dark?" demanded Seth.

"The tests are all negative" Maureen explained softly. "Everyone's in the dark."

"Want to join us for a late dinner?" Pam asked brightly, tossing back her auburn hair.

Albert nodded, but Seth shook his head no. "Tyler's parents are driving up from Atlanta. I think we need to keep watch until they get here."

"Rain check then?" Maureen asked and they all agreed.

*****

Doctor Fenn van den Bergh sauntered into Isolation 2. He caught his reflection in the mirrored door, and saw a bald emaciated man with a gray beard. The years of sacrifice to get to the top of his profession had taken their toll. The grueling drive from Baltimore hadn't helped. He gazed at the young man resting on the other side of the glass. He was young and looked strong enough to fight off this invader. The doctor punched up the tablet mounted on the glass and began to read. He tapped impatiently, navigating from screen to screen, looking for the clue. It wasn't there! He paged through the images and stopped at the cerebrum. It had an unusual caste. He had the answer to "where." "What" and "why" were still mysteries.

"I see you're still not taking care of yourself," said the familiar gentle voice behind him.

He turned and embraced his former student. "Judy," he said with a tear running down his cheek, "I'm glad you called me. I'm not sure how much I can help."

"Fenn, you're the best," protested Peterson, thinking her mentor's reply was false modesty. "If you can't diagnose it, we're in deep crap!"

Doctor van den Bergh pondered a moment, and then articulated the situation: "We are in deep crap. I've never seen anything like this! You can put a tentative diagnosis of viral encephalitis on the chart, but it's a phantom."

"Have you ever seen a virus this thermo genic?" she asked.

"Only a few tropical outbreaks," he replied. "A persistent one-hundred-six temperature that resists aspirin and aggressive cooling hasn't ever been reported. If he lives, he'll probably be twenty pounds lighter." They agreed on treatment with a broad-spectrum antiviral, until they got more information.

*****

The staff lounge was empty, which was normal for 3:30 a.m. Peterson and Doctor van den Bergh sat at a worn table, that had once been green, and talked about friends and co-workers.

"Have you thought about coming back?" Fenn van den Bergh inquired.

Peterson wondered if he had been reading her mind. Her obligation to practice in a rural community ended next year. She had been accepted, but not respected, in her current position. It seemed to be a problem of estrogen in a testosterone-rich environment. She had been thinking of the intellectual stimulation, old friends, and old romances she had left behind.

"Who wouldn't want to go back to the best medical school in the country?" she asked rhetorically. "I'm coming to the end of my indentured servitude, but I've really done some good here. We saved a lot of lives from car wrecks and hunting accidents."

"But the downside is you don't get much respect." He prompted.

She was almost in tears as she answered: "I don't expect confetti and a parade, but I saved a kid's leg last year. He twisted his ankle playing football. I treated him on the sidelines and I saw an infected toe from a previous injury. He was a day or two from sepsis. We cleared it up, but they wanted to lynch me because the kid missed the rest of the season."

"So where is the kid now?" he asked.

"On a full scholarship at Vanderbilt, but I'm banned from the sidelines!" she answered angrily.

They talked for a few more minutes, hugged, and went off to catch a few hours' sleep.

*****

Tyler lay still, breathing deeply. A small amount of liquid streamed from his left nostril, took a detour around his mouth, and dripped onto his gown.

Two

The cafeteria at the North Georgia Medical Center was a beehive of activity. Staff members were gathered in groups, talking excitedly about all sorts of subjects. Others were grabbing their lunches and rushing back to their offices.

In stark contrast, Jim Duncan calmly stared at the headline story in the *Atlanta Examiner.* The story accused a New Jersey state senator of blackmailing a Supreme Court Justice. The Justice was allegedly a frequent customer of a prostitution ring in Maryland. The State Senator threatened to expose this scandal, unless the Justice voted to uphold the End of Life regulation imposed by Health and Human Services.

The regulation would require doctors to discontinue treatment when a patient was expected to live less than a year, or if the patient had an incurable condition. A coalition of seniors' groups, pro-life doctors, and bioethicists sued to strike down the regulation. In a 5-4 decision, the Court upheld the regulation, and accepted the rationale that the decision was budgetary, designed to protect the solvency of the system. Justice Drayton voted with the majority.

Jim searched his prodigious memory. No Supreme Court Justice had ever been impeached, at least not in his lifetime. He remembered Jesus' prediction for the end times: "Even the elect will be deceived."

He reflected on his own life. After a hard-drinking college life, he had been born again as a Christian, solved his anger management issues, and became a loving husband and father. Now, in his early forties, he was confronted with temptations. Mandy, who had just been promoted to Administrator, was flirting with him. He was teaching a night course in physics. Several female students had told him, "I'd do anything to get an A in this class!" He had jokingly replied, "Try studying." Now he caught himself fantasizing about one of them. His best friend, Mark, had been a pathological womanizer. Now he was on sabbatical, working with Catholic missionaries in the Congo. It seemed their lives were reversing directions.

Jim's eye scanned back to the top of the story he had just been reading. The byline jumped out at him. It was written by Nick Polakov, a transplanted Russian, who had been a disciple of Walter Pope. Pope was the cagey reporter who stalked the halls at North Georgia Medical Center and the CDC during the prion epidemics.

The Atlanta Examiner was a red-hot newspaper founded by Diogenes Christopher, a savant in cable and internet news. Since joining the *Examiner,* Polakov had written over a dozen sensational pieces about corruption, government, and the financial industry. He had scooped his mentor on several occasions.

"You're going to rot your brain reading that trash!" growled a familiar voice behind him.

Jim sprang to his feet and embraced his former team mate. "Yoshi, what's a billionaire like you doing in a dump like this?" he thundered. "I thought you'd be on your yacht in Tahiti!"

Yoshi just shrugged. He was used to jokes about his entrepreneurial success and remembered his days as a cook in a Japanese restaurant. "I'm meeting Tony to talk about some samples he submitted," Yoshi replied.

"Anything I can help with?" Jim asked excitedly.

He had complained about the maddening stress of the prion crises robbing him of countless hours with his family. Now, he was getting bored. Doing basic research was okay, but it seemed so routine. Just set up the experiments and let the machines do the work. Mark kept telling him, "Jim, you're building the foundation for fighting the next killer epidemic."

"Have you heard from Mark?" asked Yoshi, as if he were operating on the same psychic wavelength.

Jim shook his head, "Not for a few weeks. He can only call when he's in Kinshasa, and I can't compete with Megan and the twins. Meanwhile, I'm getting fat because I don't have anybody to walk with."

"Tell me about it!" Yoshi retorted, tapping his stomach. "I'm becoming a Sumo wrestler! By the way, do you play tennis?"

"Like a golfer!" Jim answered and they both broke out laughing.

Tony DeSantis arrived, and after a few minutes of good-natured ribbing, they sat down to talk and Tony explained the situation. He had received two Level 1 samples from a small North Carolina hospital. The gross structure and DNA sequence didn't match anything in the CDC database.

"It looks like a snake wrapped around an egg roll," Yoshi said. "It's mostly helical, with small areas of beta sheet."

Tony also reported that the CDC lab was having difficulty isolating the coat protein. They all knew they couldn't interpret Yoshi's data without the primary sequence of the protein, but at least it was intact. It would not be a jigsaw puzzle like the fragmented prions.

The three scientists adjourned to the video conference suite to touch base with the CDC. The room had been state-of-the-art a few years ago during the last prion epidemic, but now that the threat was gone, the budget was cut, and the equipment was gradually becoming obsolete. Doctor Arturo Munoz, the new Director of the CDC, appeared on the enormous wall screen.

"Hi Art! Great to see you!" Tony bubbled.

"Good to see you all!" Munoz responded. "Megan is working from home today, so we're going to add her."

The screen split, and the pretty blonde lady they knew so well appeared. The screen flickered, went blank and then filled in, as the system cut the resolution to fit the bandwidth.

"You looked better in the first few frames," Yoshi quipped.

"Try chasing a pair of two year olds all day and see how you look!" Megan shot back.

The men clamored for news about Mark.

"He's been out in the bush with Father Mukana, treating brain diseases," she reported. "They're seeing a lot of West Nile and amoebic encephalitis."

Finally, after her report, they came back to the reason for the meeting.

"So far, it's only been the two cases," Megan said. "Hopefully this is just a one-off. It happens all the time. A new disease shows up, can't handle the environment, and dies off."

As they prepared to adjourn, Munoz announced, "Doctor Fen van den Bergh has asked to be on the distribution list."

They all agreed that another heavy hitter couldn't hurt.

As Tony, Yoshi, and Jim meandered into the corridor after the conference call, there was a rush of people toward the cafeteria. When asked what was happening, a technician shouted, "Judge Drayton and Senator Leonardo are holding a press conference. We could be seeing history!"

Three

The one-hundred-fifty-inch wall screen lit up the darkened theater room in the Sandy Springs condo, where Nick Polakov sat on the light tan recliner sofa with his favorite toy on his lap. The CEREBRUM was a wireless game changer. More than just a fancy digital recording device. Nick could mark up and edit the audio and video in real time. He could dictate and edit his story, research previous quotes and documents, and file his story to the paper, all without touching a key. CEREBRUM had many more features that he hadn't had time to learn. It was Diogenes Christopher's secret weapon in the media wars.

On the screen, the press conference was beginning, and the participants were being introduced. Nick jumped as he heard the phrase, "the Honorable Webster Drayton." He marked the quote as he thought to himself, we'll see just how honorable the Justice really is. Drayton gave a prepared statement denying that he had ever consorted with prostitutes, nor had he been pressured with respect to his vote. State Senator Anthony Leonardo denied any contact with Justice Drayton. Both men attacked the story as disgusting and libelous.

Leonardo demanded that Polakov be fired, and threatened a lawsuit.

Nick shook his head. *Poor bastards!* he thought. Walter Pope had constantly reminded him not to fire all his ammunition in the first salvo. These poor schmucks had no clue what was coming.

As he labored to set up his series of stories, he remembered that he owed this achievement to Aunt Ilyana. Her army of senior citizens, outraged by threats to their health care, had fed him a stream of documentation that would have made the NSA proud. There were e-mails, receipts, photos, and even surveillance videos. Almost all these sources were "on the record." Seniors felt that if the government was going to kill them, they might as well go down fighting.

Exhausted, but satisfied, he hit the recline button and began to reflect on what had led him to this apex in his career.

*****

Born Nicholas Andre Polakov, he had grown up in the shadow of the Kremlin. His father was an imprisoned dissident, so his mother was the driving force in his development. Hockey was his favorite activity, where he was a warrior with a stick, rather than a sabere. Wits and speed over muscle became his credo.

When he was twelve, his mother arranged to send Nick to America to live with her sister. The boy was fluent in English, so he adapted quickly to his Bethesda Maryland School. Aunt Ilyana guided him through two

Ivy League journalism schools. The job market, at the time of his graduation, was a great shock to him. His first job was as a copywriter at a men's fashion magazine. Undaunted, he began to network through journalism societies.

By chance, he met a young lady, whose uncle was the Sports Editor at the Washington Beacon. Nick was again hired as a copywriter. The small paper couldn't afford to pay him enough to live in Washington, so he started moonlighting as a limo driver. One night, he looked at the master schedule, and saw the name Walter Pope. Seizing the opportunity, he paid the assigned driver $25 to switch with him. "He's a lousy tipper anyway," the other driver had said with a grin. During the ride, Pope had been dictating a story.

Stopped at a red light, Nick turned and spoke to him, "I think you should lead with the paragraph about the councilman. It'll really grab the reader."

Pope had been startled, not so much at the impudence of the driver, but that the idea proved a good one. "What do you know about journalism?" he had asked defensively. Nick told him. Walter made no further comment, but began to ask for Nick as his driver.

The editor at the Beacon had begun to receive complaints about Nick. Reporters were irate that this copy editor had been doing major surgery on their stories. After comparing original and final stories, the editor, instead of censuring Nick, gruffly told the reporters to improve their writing. When Mike Pennington, a local beat reporter with a drinking problem, left the paper, Nick transferred into the opening. The demands of the new job forced him to stop moonlighting.

One day, Walter invited him to lunch at Chateau Moraine.

"I want you to work for me!" he said bluntly.

It seemed that Nick had found his dream job, big salary, great benefits, and a chance to do national reporting. It hadn't taken long for that feeling to depart. On his First monthly review, Walter had chewed him out.

"You write really well and you've got the passion, but your investigative techniques suck." Walter snapped. "Ride along with Charlie Gibbons until you prove you can do it on your own!"

Nick's pride had been hurt, but it was only the beginning. Charlie and Walter constantly berated him, while he worked 14-hour days. It was over a year before he got his own beat again. When he complained, Walter took him to task.

"You think Charlie and I are tough, wait until you work for Morrie Schoen, our editor."

Walter was right. Like a magic wand, and under Morrie's tutelage, Nick discovered the secret. Good stories attracted attention, sold newspapers, and brought in advertisers. With his new investigative skills and superior writing ability, Nick was breaking the biggest stories. As he rested on the recliner, he concluded that Walter's tough-love mentoring had made him a better journalist.

*****

Nick's contemplation was abruptly interrupted by a piercing tone from CEREBRUM. It was the encrypted phone line, a standard tool since the NSA monitoring programs were revealed in 2013. It was Stu Babcock, the Examiner's forensic accountant.

"Polakov," he barked. "I've just finished analyzing Chestnut Hill, and the other four stocks. I'm not seeing anything criminal. The statistical analysis is really sophisticated. Who's this guy that gave it to you?"

Nick chuckled, as he considered how the financial guru would react. "He's a high school kid, Stu! Next you'll be asking if I'm smarter than a fifth grader."

"So the kid's insanely intelligent. The patterns look highly coordinated. It could be a lot of average investors playing a system. As a group, they made about two-billion."

"So, how do we track down the system?" Nick queried.

"It would be tough to do," Stu explained. "The individual buy and sell transactions are too small to be reportable. Most of the systems are preproprietary, and sold to subscribers. They're not illegal."

"One thing I don't understand," persisted Nick, "what the hell is an Appledorf convergence?"

Stu sighed wearily and tried to formulate an answer. "It would take a week to explain. I had to look it up myself. It is a technique to analyze patterns. We don't use it to detect stock fraud."

"Maybe we should start," said Nick.

Stu agreed to look into it, and they called it a night.

*****

Maxine's on Roswell Road was busy for a Wednesday night. Nick liked to go there to unwind after a stressful day. The theme was French, but the clientele was a demographic mix of age, gender, and occupation. His favorite table was occupied, so he grabbed a high-top table near the bar. Gwen, his favorite waitress, automatically delivered his Bombay martini. They engaged in a little playful and meaningless flirtation. He waved to Rick, a Georgia Tech student, who was working behind the bar.

"Can I share your table?" a soft sensuous voice from over his right shoulder asked.

He spun around and beheld a young woman with expressive dark eyes, long flowing black hair, and an incredible body, showcased by a low-cut black dress. In general, there were two types of women that approached Nick; journalism groupies and hookers. If she's a hooker, Nick thought, she must be on the high end. He gestured toward the empty chair.

"I'm Sandi Meyerson," she said softly. She sat down across from him, and they exchanged small talk about the weather, food, and sports. "What do you do for a living?" she inquired.

That rules out journalism groupie, he thought.

When he told her he was a journalist, she didn't seem impressed. He asked her about her occupation.

"I'm a security analyst."

"I don't do much investing," he replied.

"No, not securities, like Wall Street," she giggled. "Security, like in crime prevention." After more conversation, he asked her to come back to his place.

"I don't kiss on the first date!" she said softly.

"So, this is a date, then," he replied smugly.

"Start counting," she said with a shy smile. They exchanged cards and parted ways.

*****

"Susie, I've hooked Tattler," Sandi spoke quietly into her encrypted phone.

"Any complications?" the National Security Director asked.

"Just one," Sandi answered calmly. "I had to rough up a couple of bangers. I couldn't surveil Tattler with a couple of punks following me!"

"Don't worry about it," Susie reassured her. "Bangers aren't going to tell anybody that a girl kicked their ass!"

They discussed the assignment, until Susie asked a question.

"How's the new rig working?"

"I'm going sleeveless and nobody has noticed." "It's a great fit," she reported.

"That's because you have the boobs to get away with it," commented Susie. "I have to wear a jacket, or everyone can tell I'm packing."

"You just have to spend a few days with Dion," Sandi counseled. "He'll fix it so it doesn't show."

"Great way to append my vacation," groused Susie.

Four

Megan had just finished pushing the twins on the swings for the third time, and she was seriously out of breath.

"Meg, you've got a call from a very hot sounding guy," chirped Karen from the patio.

Megan contemplated the irony, as she walked gingerly toward the house. How many ex-wives would show up to help the new wife when the husband was out of the country? Karen was a one-of-a-kind gem. The twins loved "Auntie Karen." She would paint pictures for them, and then hand them the brushes and a blank canvas.

"Who's on the horn?" she asked, as Karen jogged by to watch the kids.

Karen looked back and shrugged. "He wouldn't tell me," she replied.

She strolled into the living room of the old farm house and approached the antique crank phone on the papered wall. Of course, the electronic guts had been updated to state-of-the-art components. Now, she was worried. What if something had happened to Mark out in the bush in the Congo?

She picked up the cone and snapped, "This is Megan!"

"Hello Mrs. Selby," answered the disciplined voice. "This is Colonel Walters. Do you remember me?"

"How could I forget?" she replied with relief. "You're the guy that almost started World War 3!"

"Good one," he laughed. "You're the young lady that stopped me!"

"What can I do for you Colonel?" she inquired.

"I talked to your boss," his tone turning very business-like. "Your SED code is 8650. I'd like to discuss case 16503, the *Diablo* virus. It's an interesting name."

Megan flipped over to speaker, took a few steps to the antique desk, and opened file 16503 on her computer. "It's viral encephalitis," she explained. "It's called *Diablo* because of the high fever and intense delirium."

"How so?' he interrupted.

She explained the intense terror experienced by the victims, and how they described the dark figure they felt was choking them. They went over the fifteen reported cases. All the victims were adult males.

"How do you explain that?" he demanded.

"It appears to be vectored by mosquitoes. The loci are in the Smoky Mountains," she theorized. "Outdoorsmen are the most probable targets!"

Megan stared at the screen after she had hung up the phone. From her experience on the prion task force, she knew exactly what Walters was thinking. This frightening new disease could be a biological weapon, created by one of America's numerous enemies. Since the overwhelming majority of U. S. combat forces were men, a gender-selective weapon would be logical. Hopefully, since Walters had been wrong the last time, he would be more cautious.

The colonel was a member of the Joint Terrorism Task Force and, therefore, the stakes would be higher. She looked at the unconfirmed cases, and noted that fifty-eight of the seventy-one were men. In the estimation of the CDC, ninety-percent of those cases would identify as something else.

Megan stared out the back window and watched Karen teaching James and Moira about leaves. A brief pang of envy swept over her. She felt left out. Was Karen a better mother? Had Mark felt left out, and was that what had caused their marriage to fail? The antique ring tone reminded her that her job was to protect all children from voracious epidemics that seemed to be everywhere.

Her boss called to tell her about his conversation with Walters. "We've got to get a handle on *Diablo* before all hell breaks loose," he barked. "I'd like you to visit Jack Dahlkemper at the UT Experiment Station. Can you handle it?"

That stung her. She was already feeling like a bad mother. Now, Art Torres was insinuating she was a slacker. "Of course I can!" she replied indignantly. "What's he got?"

"He sorts mosquitoes by surface micro-fluorescence," Torres told her. "Tony DeSantis detected fluorescence in *Diablo's* coat protein."

"Great!" she exclaimed. "That could tell us whether it's mosquito-borne."

After she hung up from the call, she turned back to the computer to locate the site and plan the route. Maybe she could take the kids. She rejected the idea almost as fast as it popped up. Taking the twins into the epicenter of the outbreak would make her the worst mother on the planet.

That nagging phone interrupted her again. The number was unavailable, but the attribute field said "secure." She answered and a familiar voice greeted her.

"Hi Megan, it's been a few years."

The mental Rolodex spun in her brain and then she gasped, "Susie Michaels? What did I do to tick off all the national security people?"

"I know, you just got a call from our old friend Walters," Susie reassured her. "How's Mark doing in the Congo?"

"You know where he is?" Megan asked irritably. She wondered whether Susie was stalking Mark.

"We know where everybody is," Susie said ominously. "Don't worry Meg. Father Mukana has him well protected!"

Megan briefed Susie on everything she had told Walters, and Susie asked to be first in line for any new information. Megan agreed and talked Susie into giving her the secure number.

*****

By the time Megan was finished working, Karen had prepared dinner. Once again, Megan was feeling inadequate. She tried to apologize for not helping, but Karen cut her off.

"I know what a tough job you have," she said softly. "I feel really important just by helping you."

The two women sat down for dinner at the refinished oak table in the dining room. It had come with the farm-house, and was at least seventy-years old. The twins were drowsy. James nodded off and his face dropped into the mashed potatoes. Megan and Karen laughed vociferously as they cleaned him off. Megan broke the news that she had to drive up to Tennessee for a few days. Karen understood and asked if her sister could stay while Megan was away. Megan agreed immediately and hugged her again.

*****

The crickets were chirping, but everything else in the house was quiet. Karen and the twins were sleeping in their rooms. Megan was nodding off at her desk, as she tried to review one more batch of clinical reports. None of the archived encephalitis reports yielded any clue to connect to the new beast.

That annoying ring tone broke the silence, and the caller ID read Kinshasa. Megan's exhaustion instantly disappeared.

"Is that you B'wana?" she asked, using her playful salutation.

"I think so," he mumbled.

He sounded very tired and explained that they had just returned from a foray to the jungle clinics. He regaled her with stories about his expedition.

"I saw a boomslang and a Black Mamba in the trees in the same day!" he reported. "They're very poisonous snakes."

She explained her current crisis and asked whether he had seen anything similar.

"We've seen West Nile, Dengue, and hemorrhagic fevers, but nothing like what you're describing," he concluded.

Megan told him about her travel plans, but when he heard Dahlkemper's name, he got upset.

"He's a jock and a chick magnet!" he complained.

He was jealous. Enjoying the moment, she decided to tease him. "What about you, running around the jungle with all those topless women?"

He exhaled before growling his reply. "Number one, they don't go topless anymore. Number two, I go everywhere with a Catholic priest. Number three, we've got AIDS on the run, but there are still a lot of STD's."

"Those aren't the kind of souvenirs I want you to bring home," she agreed.

*****

Megan served up the blueberry pancakes and fruit. The pancakes were from a box mix, but with a few tweaks, they looked and tasted homemade. Thank God for a college roommate who majored in food science! She hugged the twins and assured them their daddy loved and missed them. She reported on Mark's phone call, leaving out the intimate parts.

"I know you hope he brings back some great pictures," Karen said brightly.

Megan kept repressing the thought, but it bubbled up again. "Is Karen still in love with my husband?"

Five

Everything was wet from the afternoon rain that had drenched the Atlanta area. Street lights cast a ghostly reflection on the deserted North Avenue pavement. Sandi lay flat on the rooftop with her omniscope, peering over the edge. It was a marvelous little device. It was an infrared telescope that could see around corners. It had a directional microphone and recorder, which could be programmed to tune out background noise. It could even be mounted on a sniper rifle to serve as a laser sight.

It had started four nights ago, after her encounter with Nick Polakov. She could almost feel the gaze of the strange man watching her from behind. She had begun to walk along the street, ducked into a darkened driveway, and squeezed into a space between a dumpster and a building. From there she changed from stalked to stalker. The man was searching for her in an X-reverse pattern. He was a pro, but not a very good one. It was almost too easy, almost like dancing.

She had tailed the Eurasian-looking man to his lair in this apartment. She began to shadow the man's two partners. They were taking turns observing Nick.

Tonight was the first night she had seen them all together in the apartment.

She sighted the lens, turned on the microphone, and hit the "record" button. After watching them swill liquor and swap obscene stories, she packed up and silently slipped down the fire escape. It would be an overcast sunrise in a half hour.

Back in her Buckhead apartment, Sandi carried out the required bug sweep, and then called Susie to file her report. She had expected to leave a message and transmit the surveillance video. To her surprise, the National Security Director answered.

"You're in early," Sandi blurted out.

"It's Iraq!" Susie explained. "Somebody tried to take out Hasani. They missed again."

"They say bullets pass right through him," Sandi recalled.

"Just a myth based on an optical illusion," Susie growled. "What have you got for me?"

"The good news is it's not a wet team," Sandi said brightly. "They're looking for one of Nick's sources. They have Russian accents, but they converse in English. I don't think they understand each other's dialect."

"Are you compromised?"

Sandi laughed so hard she could barely answer, "Not at all. The guy went off the reservation to follow me. They call me 'that hot little Sonia.' They concluded that I'm not the source."

Susie was reassured. "So what's next?" she inquired.

"I've got to take a long hot shower. I've got a lunch date with Tattler, and I smell like a moldy rooftop!"

Susie passed on one more tidbit of sage advice. "Don't get emotionally involved with this guy. It happened to me, and then the guy married somebody else. It still hurts!"

Peachtree Center was crowded with people, walking in random patterns. Sandi navigated expertly through the crush, as a running back would pass through a defensive backfield. She was wearing heels and a conservative form-fitting, navy blue dress. She scanned the entire scene, looking for individuals who didn't fit. She was packing a second .380 in her specially modified Gucci bag. Crowded places were convenient places to carry out an assassination.

She spotted Nick, who was waiting for her outside Marchant, the trendiest restaurant in Center City. He looked resplendent in a black, Armani suit and perfectly styled curly black hair. I wonder if it's for me or the restaurant, she thought to herself. She remembered Susie's admonition and went back into crowd-scanning mode.

When they got to the restaurant, she was surprised at the rock star reception they received. They walked past the waiting line and were seated immediately in the VIP section. Applause wafted around them as they followed the hostess through the crowd.

"If you set this up to impress me, it's working!" she said quietly as she took her seat.

"It's the story that broke this morning," he said nonchalantly.

Security kept autograph seekers out of the VIP section, but people within the area were asking him to sign their copies of the Examiner. Sandi saw the picture of two men dining together, and a copy of a receipt.

"Is that Justice Drayton?" she asked.

"Drayton said he never met Leonardo," he explained coldly. "This is evidence they had dinner together several weeks before the health-care decision." "So then it's over?" she asked feigning naiveté.

"No," he sighed, "they'll cite bad memory, and then vigorously attack the rest of the story!"

"So what do you do then?" she asked.

A contemplative look appeared on his face as he answered, "Walter Pope, my old boss, told me that breaking a scandal is like deep sea fishing. You hook the big fish, and it puts up a fight. You ease up and let it run, and then you yank on it again. After a few hours, the fish is exhausted. You reel it in, call the taxidermist and have the fish mounted on your wall."

"So, how many trophies do you have mounted on your wall?" she teased.

"Come over to my place and I'll show you," he answered with a sardonic smile.

The waiter delivered their drinks and took their order. Nick ordered the salmon Parisian. Sandi had thought about the braised tuna, but decided instead to order the Coq au Vin.

She had a complicated personality. She wouldn't hesitate for a split second before killing an enemy, but the thought of that poor fish, fighting for its life, disturbed her. Fish might be out of her diet for months. Their eyes were locked in a romantic gaze, but her peripheral vision was scanning the room. Gyorgi and Ivan, sitting at a perimeter table, couldn't have been more obvious if they were wearing a sign. She kept scanning. Those two clowns might just prove to be a diversion.

As they talked, she learned that Nick had a lot more material, had shared it with his editor, and that Drayton and Leonardo had no idea what was coming.

For desert, they shared an Alsace strudel, Nick paid the check, and they headed to the exit where they were swarmed by autograph hounds.

"Do you mind?" he asked Sandi, putting his arm around her shoulder.

"Enjoy yourself," she said softly, as she watched for anyone who might want something other than an autograph.

Nick suggested a visit to his office at the Examiner. It was only five blocks away, so they walked down the teeming Atlanta streets. Sandi frequently checked the rear view perspective built into her sunglasses. Not even Gyorgi or Ivan was tailing them. It was warm and humid, so they took their time.

Walking through the great, granite facade of the Examiner, Sandi was struck by the transition between the classic exterior and modern interior styles. Nick greeted the security guard, waved to a few acquaintances, and signed Sandi in as a guest. They took the elevator to the sixth floor and entered a large suite filled with manic activity. A short thin man with a curly beard strode up to them.

"Nice story Nick," he said loudly. "Where's the next one?"

Nick smiled wryly, ignoring the challenge, and made the introductions. "Ken, Sandi Meyerson. Sandi, Ken Schwartz, our managing editor."

Sandi shook his hand and sized him up. He was very young to be a managing editor, and might have AD/HD. Schwartz asked about her profession, and she replied that she was a security consultant.

"So what do you think of our security?" he asked in an argumentative tone.

"I've seen worse!" she shot back. "Your camera system is good, but their placement is less than optimal. You really need some remote locking barriers."

She handed him a business card and offered her services. Nick showed her around the offices, and then they rode the elevator down to the lobby.

As she prepared to leave, he invited her to his apartment that evening.

"Like I said, I don't kiss on the first date!" she reiterated.

"But this is our second date!" he protested.

She conceded the point, put her arms around his neck, and kissed him tenderly. As he put his arms around her, he bumped the gun nested under her armpit and took a small step back.

"Why are you packing heat?" he asked in a surprised voice.

She gave him a disarming smile, and spoke calmly, "I'm a security analyst. My job takes me into some pretty dangerous neighborhoods."

He seemed satisfied. They kissed again and agreed to meet for dinner. Susie is right, she thought, as she walked out to the street. This was going to be a tough relationship to control.

Six

This can't possibly be the right place, thought Megan, as she navigated the narrow winding driveway leading to the large two story house in the middle of the forest.

As the car turned around the last bend, a small sign announced that this was indeed the UT Experiment Station. A large outbuilding, resembling a warehouse, came into view. About a dozen people were passing between the buildings and then she saw him. He was tall, perfectly tanned, and built like a Greek god. As he sauntered through the parking lot toward the car, Megan estimated that he was in his early thirties. His silk screen T-shirt hinted at a perfect set of six-pack abs. Megan glanced self-consciously at the stubborn baby bulge that she had been unable to lose.

"Ready to go mosquito hunting?" he asked brightly, as she opened the door. He opened the rear door of the sedan and pulled out her small suitcase.

Dahlkemper showed her to her guest room, put down the suitcase, and then gave her a tour of the old mansion. He explained to her that after the collapse in federal funding, the University tried to do everything to purchase it on the cheap.

"The financial crunch has actually been good for us," he opined. "We've become better innovators. If we don't have the funds to do something the conventional way, we get creative and find a way!"

The University had taken this donated mansion, put up an inexpensive steel building, and established a multi-purpose experiment station. In the basement, Megan noticed a rather primitive, but complete fitness center.

*****

Dahlkemper was clinging to a fitness regimen that nourished his frustrated dreams. He had always been an All-American linebacker at UT, and was considered a hot prospect for the NFL draft. A collision with a Vanderbilt tight end left him with a severe concussion and a fractured neck vertebra. Pro football was not to be! He has always been a scholar athlete, so he was easily able to train as an entomologist. Subconsciously though, he kept the dream alive.

*****

The Experiment Station was Spartan, but islands of culture had sprung up. Donated art was mixed with framed scientific images. Some of the latter proudly displayed the awards they had won in the "Science as Art" contests. Most of the Station was devoted to research in forestry. Its location in the Smoky Mountains provided an ideal environment. Images of pests, diseases, and their effects in plant and animal residents of the forest were everywhere.

Dahlkemper's lab concentrated on studying ticks and mosquitoes. He showed Megan several fluorescent images of proteins on or near the surfaces of the insect bodies. Megan noted that three-fourths of the students in the lab were female. *Girls usually don't like bugs*, she thought, and wondered whether their attraction was to the science or the professor.

Dahlkemper led her into a small viewing area. He reviewed the fluoresce patterns of virus coat proteins, and then pulled up a schematic of the instrument the Station used to detect these proteins on mosquitoes.

"The trick is to achieve ultra-high amplification, and to accurately tune to the right wavelength," he explained.

He then showed her images of two mosquitoes. They both appeared to be glowing. He used a laser pointer to show the subtle differences.

"The one on the left is infected with West Nile virus. The one on the right is carrying Dengue fever. Note the difference in the wavelengths."

"So our new encephalitis would show up at a different wavelength?" Megan asked.

"Yes, Tony DeSantis found a peak at a unique wavelength," he responded, "but it might just be a goose chase. A UNC team sent six-thousand insects from the area of the first two cases. There were no matches."

"That would mean that the disease isn't transmitted by mosquitoes." she concluded.

Dahlkemper looked pensive. "That's one possibility," he mused. "It could have been a low probability bite. It might also mean that the virus kills the host mosquito."

"Those are both low probability scenarios. They're possible, so we'll have to keep on looking," Megan concluded.

Back in the mansion, Dahlkemper pulled two cold cut trays out of the refrigerator and placed them on the old oak kitchen table. Plates, silverware, and small pitchers of juice and water had already been set up. Megan was self-conscious, and picked at the fruit.

"I suggest you eat everything and load up on fluids," he said. "We're hiking the Heath Morrison trail to harvest the traps. You're going to need the carbs and the water!"

You didn't mention anything about hiking," she protested.

He smirked, "I think I mentioned comfortable shoes and casual clothes. Don't worry, it's not that far!"

He led her to a small room in the corner of the basement. Inside was a modified spray-tan booth, connected to a massive ventilation pipe. He handed her a carbon-impregnated felt mask and a pair of goggles.

"This is our universal insect repellant," he explained. "Just strip down and push the button. The nozzles will spray for five seconds. Do a slow three-hundred-sixty-degree turn. The fans will vent for five minutes. Wait until they shut off before you take off the mask and goggles." She started to object, but he cut her off. "We're going into an insect breeding ground," he snapped. "I'm not sending you back to Mark with West Nile or Lyme disease. If you want to stay here, that's your choice. I'm leaving in thirty minutes." He stalked out and shut the door. She considered her options, and curiosity overcame modesty. She locked the door, disrobed, and stepped into the booth.

*****

The fifty acres of the Experiment Station property were filled with trees, shrubs, wild fruits, and vegetables. Dahlkemper explained that a healthy forest was necessary for a healthy environment. All species were labeled with printed and computer-readable tags. They exited the grounds onto a trail. A few hundred feet into the woods, they came to a fork.

"That trail leads to a camp where we teach survival training," Dahlkemper pointed out, gesturing to the right.

He explained that the University offered a multitude of courses in order to raise money. Shortly after taking the left fork, the trail became narrow and hilly. Dahlkemper led the way to watch for hazards. The forest was home to rattlesnakes, black bears and wild hogs. Megan marveled at the muscles in this man's legs, prominently displayed by his hiking shorts. She surmised that these muscles were essential to push around huge football players.

Dahlkemper had been honest in one way. The distance to the ponds was only about a mile, but the steepness of the trail caused Megan to be totally winded. Dahlkemper, on the other hand, was not even breathing heavily. In addition, he was carrying all the equipment in his back-pack.

They finally came to the first pond, and switched out the plastic tray. One deft motion sealed the tray and injected a measured amount of carbon dioxide.

"The idea is to keep them alive, but anesthetized," he explained. He slid in the new tray and stuffed the old tray into his pack. Five more traps, and the trek back to the station, left Megan exhausted. She showered and dragged herself down to the dining room for dinner. Dahlkemper's students were milling around and applauded as Megan entered. She learned that several others, both men and women, had failed to finish the trial she had just endured. Several students sat down with her and asked about careers at the CDC. She passed out her business card and invited them to call.

The meal was simple, but creative. Wild turkey surprise with cranberry sauce was the main course. She felt like a pioneer. Dahlkemper raised his glass of cider and offered a toast.

"Megan, you're a good sport, and a science warrior!"

After dinner, they returned to the lab to evaluate their bug harvest. One by one, the trays were loaded into the sorting instrument. A tiny robot scanned the insects, picked up the ones that fluoresced, and placed them on a grid. A second robot scanned the grid and sorted the bugs by the wavelength at which they glowed. The sorting process took about two hours. There were hundreds of mosquitoes. Dahlkemper looked at the magnified grid and announced the score.

"Zip, zero, nada for Tony's spectrum. Twenty-eight positive for West Nile, and one tick with Lyme disease. We'll go hunting on the east trail tomorrow." They dispersed, disappointed but resolute. "You ought to come up and take one of our survival courses," Dahlkemper suggested, as they walked back to the mansion.

"Maybe if I ever get a vacation," she conceded.

*****

Megan was a little concerned when the ring tone clicked over to voice messaging. Where was Karen? The old farmhouse was isolated. Could something have happened? She began to leave a message when the 'call waiting' tone sounded in her ear. Megan switched over and answered.

"Meg, I'm sorry!" gasped a breathless Karen. "I was upstairs reading to the twins, and I left the portable downstairs. How's everything going there?"

"It's like going through boot camp," Megan reported. "Those mountain trails are really steep. We're doing one more day tomorrow, and I'll be home the day after."

Karen filled her in on all the fun things the kids were doing. Then she said the thing Megan wanted to hear. "The kids really miss you Meg!" A tear rolled down her cheek. Maybe her role wasn't being usurped.

After their conversation, Megan gingerly found her way into the early American period bathroom. Her legs were really sore. She washed her face, brushed her teeth, and pulled the cotton nightgown over her head. She crawled under the calico blanket on the four-poster bed, and was asleep within five minutes.

In the middle of the night, he quietly came into her room. Shirtless, he bent down to kiss her passionately on the lips. "You're the hottest woman I've ever met," he whispered softly into her ear. He gently drew back the blanket, slid his hands under her nightgown, and began to caress her body. She put her arms around his neck and explored those magnificent neck and shoulder muscles. A deep sigh escaped her lips, as she responded to his intimate touch. He began to kiss her body all over. She quivered with anticipation, longing for what was coming next.

The annoying staccato beep of her watch woke her abruptly. She moaned, this time it was because her leg muscles were killing her. "Mark, you've got to get your butt back here," she mumbled to herself. "I haven't had dreams like this since I was a teenager!"

Megan lay still to pacify her legs. She felt pangs of guilt, wanting to go back to sleep and finish the dream with Jack. As if he had picked up her psychic vibes, he firmly tapped on her door.

"Meg, your boss has been trying to reach you," he thundered. "It's urgent!"

She thanked him, and then realized that she had silenced her cell phone at dinner and had forgotten to turn it back on. She touched the E-Com key to call Art.

"What's up?" she asked. Listening intently, she took notes, then hung up and began to pack. There would be no mountain trails today.

Seven

The Mediterranean sun smiled down on the sprawling vineyard and the two-hundred-year-old palatial mansion. Vine dressers were tending the rows of the noble plants the way they had done for centuries. Claude Lemond led his forty-year-old grandson onto the stone patio. Two dour-faced security guards took up flanking positions on the grounds, out of sight and earshot. The two men sat down on comfortable chairs at a primitive stone table. Alain pulled a stack of papers from his briefcase.

"You're so serious," said the old man. He reached for the large green bottle resting in the bucket. "Have a glass of wine," he coaxed.

Alain smiled and remembered the pleasant times he had spent with his mentor, one of the richest men in the world. However, he lived in the high-pressure environment of the family business. Surely, Grosspere must understand. For over an hour, they laughed and reminisced about old times. The old man was determined to provide a place of refuge for his grandson.

When they finally began to discuss business, a copy of the *Atlanta Examiner* lay open on the table. The story of Justice Drayton was still unwinding. He had denied knowing Senator Leonardo. The *Examiner* published a photo of the two men having dinner together. Leonardo denied blackmailing Drayton. The paper retaliated with a group of e-mails referring to the Judge's habits. The denial by Drayton that he had never used escorts was refuted by a bevy of financial and photographic evidence.

The paper published Drayton's latest defense. He claimed to have decided on his vote early in oral arguments, and therefore hadn't been blackmailed. The *Examiner* promised to run a feature story tomorrow. A leader quote from the Justice's notes was displayed in a prominent font. "Denial of medical care to a terminally ill patient is abhorrent to a civilized society."

Alain pointed to the byline of the story and remarked, "I'm having that reporter shadowed. Should we take him out?"

Claude patted his grandson's arm and admonished, "Assassination is always a last resort, my boy. There must be a good reason. A plot is complex and, even if successful, the assassin owns part of you! Besides, I've been assured that Drayton's successor will be a friend."

They turned to another story on the front page. The CDC announced an outbreak of a terrifying disease. Citizens were urged to protect themselves from, mosquitoes, although a connection had not been conclusively proven.

"I received this letter from Chu," Alain said.

The old man read it and expressed concern for one of the family's most profitable businesses.

"Brauweiler is ready to publish this paper," Alain reassured him. "Here is our strategy to profit from it."

The old man smiled at the diabolic genius of it. Good old Brauweiler. They could always count on him and his colleagues to defuse a crisis.

The financial report was often a highlight of their get-togethers. Alain had learned the game well from his grandfather. The Lemond family had been bankers since the nineteenth century. Jean-Louis Lemond quadrupled the family fortune by entering international finance, and financing both sides in World War I. Claude tripled it by shorting major sovereign currencies.

Alain developed a method to manipulate stocks. He used "ghost pools," shell companies and computer programs to make the manipulations undetectable. In the last year, he had made $22 billion. His grandfather was very proud. Unfortunately, the young wizard had some bad news to deliver. Two people had been looking at a few of their trades.

"Is it anything serious?" the old man asked calmly. He had been in many sticky situations, and had handled them all.

"Probably not," the young man replied just as calmly. "They are not government people. I've had tenured professors look at the data, and they didn't see it. An average person wouldn't find it!"

"Keep an eye open," ordered his grandfather. "Remember, it was an ordinary man that uncovered the Weiss scandal!"

Alain nodded. He knew there was no comparison. Weiss had been an unsophisticated bungler. In the heat of the afternoon sun, they each had another glass of the family treasure.

Next, they discussed the plan for Alain to inherit Claude's seat at the Artemis Group.

Alain looked uncomfortable. "Explain to me again why you are choosing me, rather than my father," he questioned.

Claude sighed and pondered his reply. "Pierre is my son and I love him dearly," he answered with a rare tear in his eye, "but he is not suited to sit on the council that rules the world. He spends too much time on women and parties."

"Haven't you had your share of women and parties?" Alain inquired.

The old man smiled wistfully, remembering all the pleasures of the past. He also admired the young man's brash manner. "Women are attracted to men of wealth and power," he instructed, "but you must keep priorities at the top of your mind. You must be selective and discrete." He went on to stress the importance of these points. "You will be dealing with ruthless men, who are skilled at exploiting weaknesses and indiscretions. Your father would not survive, and he knows it!"

The young man shrugged in resignation. He knew his grandfather was right. They began to discuss the council.

"So there are eight members," the young man began.

Claude held up his hand and interrupted, "There are *ten*. Two of them are secret!"

Alain was puzzled. "Why? Who are they?" he queried.

"Perhaps they are secret so we are not confused with ten horned beast of the Apocalypse," Claude answered jokingly.

"Most likely, it is because they are in sensitive positions! Who is the leader?" Alain wanted to know.

"Everyone…none. In other words, we rotate and make decisions by consensus," Claude explained.

Alain wanted more details. "How many people work for us?"

"Millions," answered Claude, "but almost none know it. Let's just say we have a very flat organization!"

Claude began to discuss the personalities on council. "Moreau thinks he should be the leader. He claims he can trace his ancestry back to Charles Martel. No one believes him."

"How far back do we go?" asked the young man.

Claude referred him to the library, but gave him the short version. There were several name changes, but family history was filled in as far back as the Renaissance. Before that, there were several possibilities. The most probable was that they were descendants of Jewish traders, who had converted to Catholicism.

"Now, Borghese can track his bloodlines back to the Borgia family," the grandfather said seriously. "Don't accept any dinner invitations from him!" he said, clapping his hand on his grandson's shoulder.

They both laughed heartily, picturing their host poisoning their food. The old man became serious again.

"Keep a close eye on Steinberg," he warned. "He looks like a Calvinist Swiss banker, but he is a cunning, savage wolf!"

"So, we may need a woodsman to kill a wolf," said Alain grimly.

They rose to go to their rooms to wash up for dinner. They would return to Paris in the morning. Alain checked his electronic news feed from Genevieve, his personal assistant.

"The trap is set for Virosyn," he said. "Our *Examiner* reporter has a girlfriend, a hot little Sonia!"

"Don't tell your father," joked the old man, as they climbed the stairs.

Eight

It was an incredible shock to the staff, the patients, and visitors of the North Georgia Medical Center. Armed guards and metal detectors did not project the sympathetic welcoming image the hospital featured in their TV ads. The story had been all over the news, but not everyone had seen it. A female patient with colon cancer had been denied a second round of chemotherapy by the federal healthcare authorities. Doctors at the Alabama hospital claimed they were powerless to ignore the decision. The woman and her husband returned and demanded the treatment at gunpoint. A police SWAT team entered the hospital and exchanged fire with the armed couple. Casualties were three killed and eleven wounded. Ironically, the woman survived. A mob of senior citizens went wild in the streets. They threw Molotov cocktails at the hospital, at policemen and at every federal building they could find. The National Guard was called up nationwide.

For the first time since Kent State, they were issued live ammunition.

*****

The meeting had been scheduled for 9:00 a.m. It was now 9:30, and half the participants were missing. Dr. Salvador Bonea stalked in, alternately cursing in Spanish and English. The metal rods, which held his wiry frame together, had set off the detector at the front door.

"The three Stooges are running security," he griped.

The guards had detained him for fifteen minutes, until Mandy came down and sprung him. She followed him through the door and resumed her role as hostess. Jim casually sidled up to her. Even in the navy blue business suit, she managed to look incredibly sexy.

"Why are we under threat?" he asked. "We never refused to treat anyone!"

"No one knows that," she responded directly, "and we can't tell them. The feds would shut us down!"

"That's great, but where do we get the money?" he quizzed.

She dropped her voice to a low tone, which sounded even sexier. "Remember that ton of money that Susie Michaels dropped on us for the prion epidemic. There's a lot of it left."

"But how do you explain our lower mortality rate?" he said.

Now, her voice was a full throaty whisper. "I'm surprised. You're a Baptist. Don't you believe in miracles?"

*****

When nearly everyone had finally arrived, Mandy made the necessary introductions. Most of the participants knew one another. Two exceptions were doctors Fenn van den Bergh and Jamal Winston. They were covering for the absence of doctors Mark Selby and Al Jackson, who were both out of the country. Megan took control of the program, and reported on the outbreak. There were thirty-nine cases in six general locations. There were thirty-two deaths and the others were not expected to survive. One incredible anomaly was that all the patients were male. She did not mention that Colonel Walters had called repeatedly and asked to be included in the group. She noted that so far, there was no evidence of mosquito transmission.

Dr. van den Bergh was up next and presented the cases of the first two patients. He described the rapid onset, the intractable fever, and the vivid hallucinations.

"They saw the devil choking the life out of them," he commented and put up a series of charts, summarizing the subsequent cases. "The devil is in the details," quipped van den Bergh. "Thirty patients screamed about a dark animal with sharp teeth, or a dark figure that was choking them. A half-dozen had seen both. Art, you made an appropriate choice, naming this monster the *Diablo* virus," he concluded.

Extensive discussions broke out regarding the runaway fever and the hallucinations. A question arose as to whether the fever might be related to unexplained cases of spontaneous combustion. Debate then focused on the significance of hallucinogenic images. Some thought it was in the optic nerve, others argued for the cerebral cortex. One person suggested demonic possession. Since there was no consensus, they broke for lunch.

*****

Jim sought out a table near a corner of the noisy, chaotic cafeteria. By nature, he was not anti-social, but lately he had been feeling moody and pensive. Mandy set down her tray and sat down next to him.

"Woman trouble, or is this crisis getting to you?" she asked softly. He wasn't ready to share, particularly with the person at the center of his emotional turmoil. She put her hand on his arm and persisted. "My brother came back from the war in Afghanistan with PTSD. He was moody and withdrawn; felt like he didn't fit in. The family helped him pull out of it. I'm not going to let you go over the edge!"

He was both reassured and alarmed. The guilt over his lust for her welled up again. "Thanks," he mumbled softly as he smiled at her.

She smiled back and changed the subject. "Are you buying the demonic possession theory?" she teased.

He thought for a moment, and then gave a pensive response. "I believe there's an evil force, but I'm a scientist, and I look for data. I think the Catholics have it right. They exclude every other possibility before they consider an exorcism."

*****

Megan found herself in the middle of a heated lunch hour debate. She was seated between Fenn van den Berg and Jamal Winston who were intensely arguing about the Supreme Court's healthcare ruling. Megan was catching a few droplets of saliva from both directions. She was afraid that a food fight would break out at any moment. Van den Bergh insisted the regulation was necessary.

"The statistics are clear," he argued. "The last year of life is the most expensive by far. At some point, you have to let people die!"

Winston scowled, and responded in his melodic Jamaican tone that disguised his anger. "The Hippocratic oath compels us to use our best efforts. I have seen patients survive terminal brain tumors."

"How many?" van den Berg demanded. "Two or three," Winston retorted angrily, "but multiply that by all the neurologists in the country. Would you sacrifice them all to save money?"

Megan sensed this debate could go on all day, with no solution. She raised her hand and announced it was time to reconvene the meeting.

*****

Everyone had the age old tendency to nod off after lunch, but as soon as Tony DeSantis put up the first image, the audience snapped back to full attention. The protein coat of the *Diablo* virus looked like a misshapen serving of caviar. The component shapes began to change colors as the image rotated.

They had all seen it before. Tony had published online a month ago. On the giant screen, however, it was much more dramatic. Tony switched to split screen and brought up a second image for comparison.

"As you can see, it bears a resemblance to the meningitis NIC virus," he lectured.

Questions began to fly like snowballs. Why was the fever so high? Were there any clues to the mechanism of transmission? If it was meningitis, why didn't it show up in the spinal fluid?

Jamal snapped his fingers. "Nasal transmission!" he shouted. "The nose is their highway to the brain!"

It was an answer no one wanted. It meant the virus had probably gone airborne.

*****

Dr. Shu Ling regaled the group with models of *Diablo's* DNA structure. Again, the images and sequences resembled meningitis NIC, but the size was larger.

"These are the extra strands," Ling noted, as he flipped through seven more screens. He paused at the last image. "This one looks very familiar," he said with a frown, "but I just can't place it!"

There was a murmur of agreement from the group. Valerie Price, a special guest and Tony's better half, suggested several targets for antibody development. The group plotted their next steps and then adjourned.

*****

Fenn van den Bergh sought out Jamal Winston in the post-meeting rush. "Jamal, would you please join me for dinner," he began. "I'd like to discuss the clinical data with you in more detail."

Jamal hesitated for a moment, remembering their heated argument at lunch but, the old man was an international known neurologist. Perhaps together they could come up with some critical insights. He accepted the invitation.

"Good!" van den Bergh said, "I hope I can convince you that I'm not a callous monster. Occasionally, reality blinds me to the power of idealism."

*****

Megan was picking up scattered papers from the podium when, in her peripheral vision, she caught sight of Mandy and Jim in the back corner of the room. Mandy was stroking his arm. It looked like she was trying to comfort him. Megan shook her head. *First Mark and now Jim*, she thought.

"Hey pretty lady, you didn't invite me to your party," a familiar voice said from behind her.

Startled, she spun around to face a grinning Jack Dahlkemper. "I didn't know you were going to be here," she stammered. "Otherwise, I would have dragged you in. What brings you to the neighborhood?"

"I brought some mosquitoes with some strange spectra for Tony to play with," he replied. "Besides, I'll let you bring me up to date over dinner!"

She thought about the dream combined with her current vulnerability, and proposed a safer alternative. "If you're heading back to Tennessee, why not have dinner at my house?"

He agreed to follow her home. Megan turned off the lights, locked the doors, and dashed off a text to Karen. "Put on your best dress. Bringing a guest for dinner!"

The two cars pulled into the driveway. Gravel crunched beneath tires as they approached the massive old farmhouse. The exterior lights fed energy to the trees, which cast dancing shadows across the grass, mottled earth patches of red clay. Karen opened the front door to let them in.

"My God, is she gorgeous," Megan gasped under her breath. The long flowing blonde hair, the flawless complexion, and the sleeveless black dress showing a teasing bit of cleavage were all perfect. Megan introduced them. She could tell that Jack was impressed. Megan felt a twinge of jealousy, and told herself, *I'm going to have to up my game before Mark comes home!*

The twins came bouncing in, but ran to hide behind Megan. They had never seen a man so big and so muscular. He finally coaxed them out and picked them up, with one perched on each massive shoulder.

"Now you're as big as I am," he chuckled. "Nieces and nephews," he said to the ladies. Jack gave them a ride into the dining room, right behind Karen.

Over Megan's protests, Karen slipped on an apron and began to serve the salad. "You've had a rough day and you need to relax," Karen softly chided.

She even looks great in an apron, thought Megan. They talked about life, nature, and played with the kids, while scarfing down the Beef Bourgeon, green beans, and apple pie. Karen smiled approvingly as Jack passed on anything alcoholic. She excused herself to take the twins upstairs despite their protests. They wanted to stay and play with the gentle giant.

"She's quite a lady," Jack remarked. "Did you find her through an agency?"

His jaw dropped when Megan explained that she was Mark's first wife. "Unbelievable!" he quipped, "Professor Selby never taught us how to find women as beautiful as you two!"

Megan wasn't sure whether she was blushing from the wine or the compliment. She began to update him on the epidemic.

"Seems like two mysteries," he observed while stroking his stubbled chin. "Why does it only infect men, and what's going on with these weird hallucinations?"

"Maybe demonic possession?" she joked.

He scowled and responded thoughtfully, "I wouldn't discard that possibility too quickly. Have you ever seen a Christian snake handling ritual? They do everything to provoke those rattlesnakes, but they're hardly ever bitten. Have you ever seen someone die from a voodoo curse?"

Megan was horrified, not sure whether he was returning the joke. "Is that scientific?" she queried, barely above a whisper.

"Just because we don't understand something, it doesn't mean we can't consider it," he reasoned.

Jack declined her invitation to stay overnight in the guest room. He had to meet with a survival class at 7:00 a.m. She fretted about him driving the curving mountain roads in the dark. He reassured her that he was at home in the mountains, day or night. At the door, he impulsively leaned down and kissed her, and thanked her for dinner. She closed and double-locked the door. She was having vivid visions of zombies and voodoo rites.

The text alert on her phone made her jump. It was from Tony who as usual, was working late. There was a link and a short note.

"Read this paper by Brauweiler. It looks like the answer!"

Nine

Tony DeSantis was puzzled. He had determined DNA and protein coat structures on the *Diablo* viruses from all reported cases. CDC had confirmed these structures down to the last detail. Brauweiler had published an urgent communication online. His research group in Switzerland had incubated meningitis virus with Synovir's anti-virus drug S-1460. A new virus appeared, having the same coat protein structure as *Diablo*. It was puzzling that the DNA structure was different. How could that be? The DNA determines the protein structure. He had handed the problem over to the Emory supercomputer whiz kids, but they told him it would take about a week. Tony was an impatient guy, and he hated waiting for answers. He started taking notes on the gross structural differences. The first difference that jumped out at him was the DNA strand that everyone thought was so familiar. It wasn't there in Brauweiler's structure.

After three hours of note taking, Tony was so focused that he didn't notice that the love of his life had strolled into the lab.

"Forget about lunch?" she inquired in an annoyed, but understanding, tone.

"God! Is it that late already?" he shouted in disbelief, glancing at his watch.

Valerie gave him a stern look, "If you've changed your mind, I have a standing invitation to go walking with Jim!" she teased.

He broke out laughing and threw his arms around her. She always cracked him up, this cute Vietnamese orphan with the southern accent she had acquired from her adopted family.

"You're out of the loop, now that you don't work here anymore," he chuckled. "Jim walks along the river with Mandy now!"

Valerie was surprised. Jim was a straight arrow religious guy, while Mandy had a reputation as a readily available sex crazed woman.

Tony kissed Valerie affectionately.

"For old times' sake?" she giggled, looking toward the closet.

"In the closet?" he asked. "You're crazy!"

They walked toward their rendezvous closet, as she began to unbutton her blouse.

Their clothes were slightly disheveled as they sat together in the manic atmosphere of the North Georgia cafeteria. No one noticed their appearance in an environment where rumpled clothing was a sign of working long hours. They had planned for a romantic lunch at McGrath's, but their forty-five minute interlude sentenced them to cafeteria food.

Jim and Mandy, who had just returned from their walk, joined them.

"It looks like the Swiss have scooped us," babbled Mandy, anxious to avoid any conversation about her new relationship with Jim. "They had quite a show at their press conference, and it looks like the FDA is going to move on S-1460!"

"I'm not so sure," Tony responded haltingly. "They were pretty sloppy about interpreting their details."

Mandy nodded and sprung her surprise, "Art called this morning, and CDC is having their own press conference at five-thirty. Etienne is sending Jamal. Tony, can you go and represent the basic science side?"

Tony hated the press. They just whipped up emotions and confused everyone. He agreed reluctantly, and made a mental note to change his shirt.

Back in the lab, Tony laid out all the discrepancies in Brauweiler's DNA structure. "I wish I could remember where I've seen that strand that's missing," lamented Tony.

"I know," Valerie said soothingly, putting her arm around his shoulders. "I've seen it before too, but I couldn't find it in any of the neuroviruses in my files." She had to run back to her own lab for a meeting. She kissed him tenderly. "See you at home?"

"Absolutely," he reassured her. "I just don't know when this pain in the ass press conference is going to end."

Tony's text alert sounded the trumpet call from Churchill Downs, which called the race-horses to the gate. It was from Jim, and it reported, "Finding a crazy alpha structure in lipids from infected brain tissue." Tony trotted three doors down the hall and burst into Jim's lab. "You couldn't walk a few feet and tell me personally!" he shouted in mock anger. "What's it mean?"

"Damned if I know," Jim replied softly. "Maybe it explains why the brain turns to jelly when it's infected. I sent a text because I didn't want to disturb you and Val. I know you two hadn't had much time together."

Tony's face flushed. Now he was relieved that Jim hadn't come by his lab at twelve-thirty. "You just didn't want to face Valerie's wrath," Tony countered. "She's jealous that you left her for another walking partner!"

Now it was Jim's turn to blush. "Got to walk with somebody or I'm going to get fat," he said defensively. They laughed and went back to talking technology until Tony had to leave.

*****

Megan was going out of her mind trying to prep for the press conference. She had tried to get Art to just put out a press release, but he told her Washington was insisting on a full blown dog and pony show. He also assured her that he had her back. Fen, Jamal, and Tony would carry most of the load. CDC's position was that they were studying the Swiss results, and would continue to work with their partners to clarify the facts.

Her ears were still burning from the conversation she had with Sir Roderick Booth, the CEO of Synovir. He had been blindsided by the Swiss report, and claimed that business rivals were trying to destroy his company.

He went on further to attack Brauweiler's reputation, and to describe him as a hired gun. She assured him that everyone working with CDC would attempt to repeat the experiment, and would be completely fair. He totally lost it, screaming that Synovir had lost fifty-percent of its value in one day. She just didn't know how to console the man.

Fenn van den Bergh was the first to arrive at the press room. Megan greeted him and gave him a brief orientation. She showed him the line-up and asked if he wished to make an opening statement. He shook his head.

"I'm too old, and I ramble too much."

"Fenn, do you know Brauweiler?" Megan asked.

Fenn chose his words carefully. "They call him the Renaissance man," he mused. "It's not a compliment. He gets his money from very wealthy private donors. He's become a very wealthy man."

Megan tried to get more. "Do you think he could be a hired gun?"

"I've heard rumors, but I never believe them. Someone would have exposed him by now."

The other presenters began to filter in. The press was filling up the adjacent room. Megan spotted Walter Pope, with whom she had a less than pleasant history. Pope was conversing with a younger man, who was accompanied by a stunning brunette.

"Why am I running into so many women who make me look like a plain Jane?" she asked God.

On the dot, the press was let in and the soap opera began. The press wanted someone to blame, but Art wasn't having any of it. He laid down the rules of decorum. No questions until all the presentations were complete. CDC presenters would only discuss facts, and not indulge in speculation. They would not discuss actions where cases were in the purview of other bodies, such as the FDA.

Megan took control of the program and presented status. Art had to step in to silence the murmuring. Jamal presented the symptoms and progression of the disease: high intractable fever, violent hallucinations, and death. He solicited comments from van den Bergh, who had treated the first patient. Megan glanced through the window to the hallway and noticed Sandi, continually looking to the right and left. *I wonder what she's looking for,* Megan thought.

The gallery exploded as Art opened the floor for questions. The first series focused on the name *Diablo*. Did it have something to do with the occult? Would exorcism help? The normally quiet van den Bergh took the question head on.

"We don't live in the Dark Ages!" he responded loudly. "We could do an EEG and thermography to find out what part of the brain is affected, but that is not a priority. There's no evidence these patients are being scared to death."

Walter Pope asked about the apparent sex selectivity of the disease. "Could it be a biological weapon?"

Megan gasped and rolled her eyes. "Not again," she whispered, recalling how close they were to Armageddon only a few years ago.

Art stated that there was no evidence and no one should speculate. Polakov asked about the Swiss report, and the role of the drug S-1460. Tony pointed out the discrepancies in the DNA structure and stated that more evidence was needed before attributing the epidemic to the drug. Art shot Tony a malevolent glare as all hell broke loose. Questions were flying wildly. What were Tony's qualifications? Was he questioning the competence of the Swiss scientists? Was he suggesting that the FDA should not pull the drug?

Tony calmly clarified his conclusions. "There is a major difference in the origins of the samples. One was from an actual patient, while the other was derived from a different virus in the laboratory. It should be no surprise to any of us that there would be differences."

After the press had fully vented their fury, Art thanked them and concluded the proceedings.

Megan found Tony and put her hand on his shoulder to comfort him. "Wow, you really know how to liven up a press conference!" she teased.

"Meg, what did I do wrong?" he lamented.

"Absolutely nothing," she said soothingly, stroking his shoulder. "You had the most logical presentation. These people don't respect logic. They want drama and controversy. Don't ever give it to them!"

"What's going on here? Are you trying to steal my girl?" Megan and Tony heard a voice behind them and turned to face Mark.

Their jaws dropped. He had lost about twenty-five pounds, his face sunken, and his eyes protruding.

"Oh my God, what are you doing here?" Megan squealed, throwing her arms around him.

"Susie Michaels and Etienne insisted that I come back a month early to handle a national crisis here. Can't you handle anything without me?"

Megan began to cry. "You don't look like you would have survived another month!" she sobbed. "What happened to you?"

"Western digestive systems are no match for African microbes," he quipped.

Megan put an arm around his waist, led him out to the car, and drove him home.

*****

The headlights on the Nissan were playing hide and seek with the twisting North Georgia mountain road. An occasional area of red clay showed itself where the rocks had fallen away from the side of the mountain. Mark and Megan chattered excitedly as they tried to catch up on the five months they had been apart. He asked about her trip to the Tennessee Experiment Station.

"Dahlkemper really is a jock," said Megan, "what a body!"

"I was a jock," Mark interjected defensively.

"You played tennis!" Megan pointed out, snickering.

"NCAA Division One tennis!" he shot back.

Megan knew she was making him jealous. "Relax, I tried to set him up with Karen," she giggled.

"He's not right for her either," he opined moodily.

Now it was her turn to be jealous, so she decided to stop teasing. It was so great to have him home safely!

It was late and everyone was sleeping. They quietly snuck in the front door, reactivated the security system, and tip-toed upstairs. She helped him out of his clothes and escorted him to the shower. She did an enticing strip tease and stepped into the shower with him. He was already aroused, even though exhausted from the all day trip. They playfully soaped each other all over, rinsed, and quickly dried off. They were still damp when they rolled into the brass four-poster bed. They were way past ready and made passionate love. She had never been a screamer, but, on this night, it took an extreme effort to hold back. She had not experienced multiples for almost three years. Afterwards, he was exhausted and fell asleep in minutes. She lay with her head on his rhythmically rising and falling chest, wondering whether they had just created another pair of twins.

Ten

Nick and Sandi sat on the couch looking over the newsfeeds from the overnight wire. Carry-out containers and half empty coffee cups littered the living room table, a contrast to the rest of Nick's well-kept condo.

The morning meetings had become a ritual to allow her more time to plan his security. She had secretly installed five miniature ST-1200 sensors in and around his unit with a direct feed to her communicator. She could now guard him from a distance. Why then was she having this uneasy feeling? The Russian shadow team had stopped following them, but they were still in town. So what was bothering her? Maybe it was that she was beginning to have deep feelings for this guy. He was good looking, aggressive, and had a zest for life. His most attractive feature was that he cared deeply about people. She could see it when he was working on stories where corruption was hurting someone.

Nick's voice broke through the silence. "Drayton is holding a press conference, and speculation is that he's going to resign!" She put a hand on his shoulder and congratulated him. His face tightened into a scowl. "I feel bad for the old guy," he groused. "You know, I was reading through his decisions for background, and a lot of them were great. He really knew the law, but he always seemed to base his decisions on fairness. I guess he was a lonely guy who got caught up in patronizing escorts. If he had just told the truth, I wouldn't have had to filet him on the front page."

"He probably didn't want to embarrass the Court," she suggested.

"It didn't work" he said sourly. "Now, how can people ever trust his words again?"

The ring tune was unusual, but Nick recognized it immediately. It was unusual for Stu to be calling this early. He was a night person.

"Stu, what have you got?" Nick asked in his staccato phone voice.

Stu's voice was shaking. "The kid just sent me a list of over a thousand stocks that are being manipulated," he began. "He said someone is trying to hack his security system, and he's not going to send us any more stuff. Maybe he's making me paranoid, because I could swear there are guys following me."

Sandi was good at maintaining a poker face, but Stu had answered one question for her. What happened to the gang that couldn't shoot straight? It was a cardinal rule of spy craft. If the person you had under surveillance saw you, you were doing a lousy job.

"Let's trim that list back to five stocks," Nick suggested and Stu enthusiastically agreed.

"Fine, we'll pull out the top five with the highest Appledorf values, and then we'll try to untangle the trades and follow the money."

Sandi and Nick picked up the remains of their deli breakfast. Sandi enjoyed these get-togethers and they were helping her do her job. He was sharing his work with her, and that knowledge could help her identify the potential threat. The down-side was that she had put on the pounds by eating all that rich food. Fortunately, she was in great physical shape and the extra weight didn't show. Unfortunately, the ex-Marine in her brain told her that someday she might have to drag those extra pounds over a wall. As an agent, she knew that her holster was designed to her shape, and those extra pounds might slow her reflexes by a fraction of a second. Maybe she and Nick could start working out together.

They picked up their briefcases, took the elevator to the street, and walked to the MARTA station. Sandi made sure to make them late, so they would miss his habitual train. She knew that the key to a successful assassination was planning. It's essential for potential targets to change their schedules. Sandi's job was more difficult, because she had to get him to do it without telling him why. It was bad enough that he would be at every press conference.

Arriving downtown, she convinced him to walk by Bakers to check out the window display. It took them three blocks away from their normal routine. When they got to the paper, she kissed him and promised to meet him at Justine's at six-thirty that evening. As she turned to leave, she spotted a familiar figure leaning against a building down the street. Gyorgi hadn't followed them. She made a mental note to find out whether he was shadowing Stu.

*****

Back at her apartment, she made her customary bug sweep, and then dialed up Susie on the highly encrypted phone. She reported that the Russians may have switched to following Stu and that it might be related to a story about stock manipulation.

Susie whistled and remarked. "If this involves thousands of stocks, that's a ton of money. That would be a motive to kill!"

Susie reported that the three Russians were low-level mob guys who were normally collectors and couriers. It would be a big jump for them to pull off a hit. Sandi was insulted.

"They didn't even have the respect to send professionals!"

She told Susie that she would confirm that Stu was the new surveillee. They signed off, and Sandi sat down at her desk to disassemble her gun. It had been windy and dusty on the street.

*****

Sandi caught a bus downtown. It was the middle of the afternoon, so she had no trouble finding a seat. Seeing nothing suspicious, she focused on the young girl holding a beautiful baby. Her thoughts went back to her life at that age.

She wanted badly to be a wife and mother. When she met Lou, she knew that he was the one. Then one day she told him that she had missed a period, and the next he was gone. It was a false alarm, but she wondered if she could have been like that young girl. Sandi was disturbed when the girl turned her head, revealing a black eye. Sandi moved up to an adjoining seat and began a conversation with her. When asked about the eye, she spouted the usual story about walking into a door.

You'd think they could come up with something more original, thought Sandi. She tried to convince her to seek help, but the girl seemed too afraid. As a last resort, she gave the girl her cover card and told her to call if she didn't feel safe. As Sandi got off the bus, she had no idea what she would do if that call ever came.

Sandi checked her encrypted phone for the list of numbers she had secretly lifted from Nick's phone. She found Stu's number and dialed it on the disposable she had picked up two days prior. When he answered, she introduced herself as Carla.

"The people at your paper told me that you're the man to talk to about exposing stock fraud," she said softly.

She elaborated a story about a group of investors who were colluding to rig stock prices. She asked about a reward, and he explained the whistle blower bounty.

"You could get a percentage of the amount recovered, if someone is convicted," he told her.

She arranged to meet him at the Phoenix Coffee Shop, two blocks down the street. She watched patiently as Stu exited the front door of the *Examiner,* and headed down the street. Gyorgi began to tail him. Just to be sure,

Sandi became the caboose on the train and followed them both. She observed them enter the Phoenix, order coffee, and sit at tables on opposite sides of the room. So, now, she knew this was connected to the stock fraud story. Stu would conclude that his no-show informant had gotten cold feet.

Now Sandi had to hurry. She had to hop on the bus, get back to her apartment to shower and primp, go back downtown, and meet Nick at Justine's by six-thirty.

Her cover phone rang while she was on the bus. She was relieved that it was Nick, and not that young girl. He told her he had commandeered a company limo, and that it would pick her up at six o'clock.

"I wanted to make this a special night," he proclaimed.

Her pulse was racing. She had known this night would come, and dreaded it. They had not been intimate yet, and Nick had been very patient. She had had unemotional sex before as part of an assignment, but this was different. She was getting close to this guy, almost as close as she had been with Lou. In fact, Nick was kind and considerate, while Lou was arrogant and abusive. Could it be a maturity thing? Was it because Nick was successful and Lou had a long run of failure? She slapped her head to restore reality. Getting involved romantically could compromise her judgment in a life or death situation.

The *Examiner* limo was stocked with a full bar. She sipped a half glass of merlot so she could remain calm, but sober and professional. At Justine's, people stopped and stared as the doorman took her hand to help her from the limo. She was beautiful enough to be a movie star. The doorman even declined the tip she offered. Nick strode down the steps and took her arm. Several cameras were flashing as they walked to the front door.

Nick had pulled out all the stops to get the nicest private table in the restaurant. The head waiter introduced himself and summoned the wine steward, who suggested several vintages. They selected a Rothschild cabernet. The menu was extensive and took almost ten minutes to peruse. Sandi pointed out a dish to Nick and they both giggled like teenagers. Whoever knew that pigeon would be so expensive? They decided to split an escargot with a pickled beets appetizer. The onion soup looked good, but they couldn't decide on the main courses. The waiter talked them into the flaming filet mignon, New Orleans style.

"We get our beef from Pine Mountain," he bragged.

They ordered and the waiter hustled off.

"Stu got a tip today from a lady who said she had information about stock fraud, but she was a no-show," Nick remarked.

"She's here in Atlanta?" Sandi asked, feigning interest.

Nick explained that Stu tried a trace, but it was a disposable phone.

"If she's involved, she's probably scared," Sandi suggested.

The steak arrived, flaming on an iron platter. The heat was so intense; Sandi thought her lipstick would melt. Once the flames went out, the waiter expertly carved the smoking filet. It was extremely tender, and spiced in the Cajun style.

Pleasantly full after the main course, they sipped their café au latté and waited for their raspberry tart desserts. Nick gave a sign to the waiter, meaning they didn't want to be disturbed. He leaned over the table and pulled a small velvet case from his pocket.

"Sandi Meyerson, I've decided that I love you," he said softly, snapping open the case to reveal a Cartier ruby in gold setting.

Sandi was stunned. "This is very sudden and very soon, but very beautiful," she stammered.

"Sandi," he said softly, "I'll slip this on your finger if you care about me. If you're not where I am yet, we'll call it a friendship ring."

She didn't say a word, but just held out her hand.

*****

The limo drove through the shadows of the lights on Peachtree. Sandi sat silent, resting her head on his shoulder. What the hell am I doing? she thought. He doesn't know who I really am. She was still keeping a close watch on the driver, the surrounding cars, and the people on the sidewalk. Now she could chalk up one more reason to keep him alive.

Back in Nick's condo, they relaxed, kissing passionately on the couch. She gently put her arm under his arm, which was around her waist, and slowly guided it. He began to caress her breast, and simultaneously unzip her dress. Suddenly, he pulled back and laughed. Sandi was shocked and irritated.

"Can we do something with the gun?" he chuckled. "It's a little intimidating!"

She started laughing. "Sorry," she exclaimed, as she stood up, slipped out of the dress, and placed the holstered pistol on the coffee table. "You know I feel naked without my gun," she teased.

"That's what I was hoping for," he responded, sweeping her up in his arms and carrying her toward the bedroom.

On the coffee table, Nick's phone clamored in vain for attention. The text message from Stu was marked "Urgent." It would have to wait patiently until morning.

Eleven

Voices were murmuring in the antique room, but ceased abruptly as Claude and Alain Lemond strolled through the door. Alain looked up and saw it for the first time. On the unfinished oak wall hung a solid gold figure of a beautiful woman, standing at the ready with a bow and arrow. It was Artemis, the Greek goddess of the hunt. She was over 200 years old, almost as old as the group of powerful men that bore her name. Throughout history, the group had built and destroyed men, companies, and countries, all in the name of profit. In this respect, they were like the gods of Olympus. Like Artemis, they would hunt, stalk prey, and then fire the lethal arrow. This week it had been Synovir. Shorting the stock had netted them $600 million.

The men assembled to take their seats at the long, mahogany table that could have been crafted during the Renaissance. There were no hearty greetings or handshakes. As bound together as these men were by the cult of wealth and power, they neither trusted nor liked one another. Just because you were at that table on that day, did not mean you would be there for the next meeting.

Two speakers were wired up at the end of the table to accommodate the two secret members. The disembodied voices announced they were ready to proceed. Alain's trained ear determined that one was Eastern European, possibly Hungarian. The other was Chinese, likely Mandarin.

Moreau called the meeting to order. The first item on the agenda was the accession of Alain Lemond to his grandfather's position on the Council. This was an unusual, but not unprecedented situation. Two members expressed concern about this generation skip. When Claude and Alain were given a chance to respond, Claude assured them that Pierre Lemond had voluntarily agreed to step aside in favor of his son. Alain cited his string of successes managing the Council's investments.

"Can you assure us that you will not discuss the business of the Council with your father?" Moreau demanded.

Alain faced him squarely and responded, "My grandfather has been my mentor. I swear, in the presence of God, that he is the only person with whom I will discuss these matters."

He knew the invocation of God was only for dramatic effect, since all these men were atheists.

When the vote was taken, eight members voted to accept Alain. Only Moreau and the Chinese member abstained. They got up to shake his hand and welcomed him as a member. He sensed it was the last friendly act he would see from this group.

They proceeded to the only other item on the agenda, the civil war in Nigeria. Alain sat impassively as the others argued back and forth whether the government or the rebels should be victorious. Alain didn't care who won. His role would be to supply both sides, prolong the war, and maximize the profit. His smart assistant vibrated to alert him that he had an urgent text. His blood ran cold as he read the alert. *Damn it*, he thought, *an American high school kid*! *They are all supposed to be drug-crazed idiots.* He noticed that his grandfather was glaring at him. The old-timers didn't appreciate electronic devices in their meeting, at least since the American NSA scandal a decade ago. The debate wrapped up and the decision was made to support the government. The rebels were ideologues and might not be agreeable to allowing exploitation of their natural resources.

After the meeting was formally adjourned, Alain approached a large, bespectacled man with a gaunt pale face. "Herr Steinberg, I need your assistance with a delicate matter," Alain said.

The old man looked at him searchingly. "It will cost you," he responded flatly.

"If this is not handled properly, it will cost us all!" Alain shot back sharply.

He went on to explain the situation.

"Wunderkind," Steinberg commented, amazed at the predicament the young man had gotten himself into. "Perhaps we should have inducted him into the Council!"

Alain winced at the stinging sarcasm. It was only his first meeting, and already he had made an adversary that he knew he would have to get rid of someday.

"You handled that well," his grandfather counseled him in the car, "but, when you are treated with disrespect, don't display your anger. You almost had it right. Remember, you are young and he is old. The day will come when you will dominate the Council."

*****

It was pandemonium for breakfast. The twins were climbing all over Mark as he tried to eat his bacon, eggs, and toast. He accepted their affection happily. It hadn't gone so well the first two days. After not seeing their dad for five months, the kids weren't sure he was a trusted adult. Maybe it was that he looked older and more frail. Finally, they realized that daddy was home. If only it could work out as well for the adults!

There was an uneasy truce among them. He thought it was an ideal arrangement, having Karen in the house to help with the kids. Megan was feeling insecure. "I hope you're not getting any ideas about a threesome," she had told him the previous day. He tried to relay what Father Mukana had said to him. There are two kinds of love between people according to the Greeks, *Eros, and Phila. Eros* was a carnal or sexual attraction, while *Phila* was a spiritual or platonic love. He reassured Megan that he felt both for her. With Karen, it was only *Phila.* She seemed to accept that. It wasn't all bad though. She was wearing him out in the bedroom, just in case.

*****

Megan's business phone rang insistently. The tone indicated it was from the Main Conference Room at the CDC. She flipped the switch to forward it to the screen. The picture was filled with people. Counting noses, the whole team was there, plus a few more.

"I didn't know we had a team meeting scheduled for today," Megan began.

"We didn't," Art replied. "This is an emergency session that we put together in the last hour. Mark, Susie Michaels called and requested that you take over leadership of the team."

Mark was stunned. "Tell Susie to take a flying leap!" he shouted. "Megan's doing a great job, and as far as I'm concerned, it should stay her team!"

"Thanks for cleaning that up for family viewing," Art laughed. "That's what I already told her, plus I added that Meg has my full confidence!"

"So then, what's the emergency?" Megan queried.

Art called on Tony to break the news. Tony took the floor just to introduce his colleague, Sara Bellamy from the Emory super computer center. She put up the slide showing the now familiar structure of the *Diablo* virus.

"Tony asked me last week to examine the data from the Brauweiler group's communication and compare the results. What the University discovered is this is our picture."

"You mean they confirmed our results and found it was the same structure," Mark prompted.

"No," she replied firmly, "What I mean is that this is our picture! Someone copied Tony's picture and relabeled it!"

This revelation stunned everyone on the team. It was an accusation of blatant scientific fraud. They began clamoring for proof. Sara maneuvered the pointer to lasso a small region of the photon and then began to zoom in on it.

"This little thin line is just barely visible," she explained. "At first, we thought it was an artifact. But when we blew it up, we found these one-hundred-sixteen pixels. If you compare them to our photo, they have the exact composition as our label. What they did was air brush out Tony's label, and substituted their own."

Silence persisted for a few minutes to allow the group emotion to shift from disbelief to indignation. "We've got to report this to the FDA and the World Health Organization!" Tony shouted angrily. "They've got everyone looking in the wrong direction!"

"No!" shouted Megan. "I'm asking everyone on this team not to say a word about this to anyone else. We've got to find the answer to one basic question. Why did they do it?"

Mark gazed at his wife in amazement and admiration. Her logic was so clear and straightforward. "When did you morph into Susie Michaels?" he asked softly.

"Great point Megan!" Art blurted out. "No sense letting them know we're on to them. Let's get a complete list of Synovir's competitors in the antiviral drug area. Then let's see if any of them are funding Brauweiler."

"You won't find out," objected van den Bergh. "He keeps his donors secret."

*****

Sara was packing up her notes and preparing to leave the podium, when she had an afterthought. "Oh Tony," she shouted over the din of conversation. "You asked me to identify that familiar looking strand of DNA. It's human, likely female."

The team reacted as if Sara had thrown a hornet's nest into their midst. Everyone was trying to talk at once. When Art finally restored order, Mark summarized the contradiction.

"The sole reason a virus infects a human cell, is to force it to produce viral DNA, not the other way around."

Tony suggested that the samples might contain DNA from the patient. Megan shot a hole in that theory, by pointing out that all the patients had been male. Nevertheless, Sara's data suggested that this strand had a female origin. Silence fell over the group as they hit a dead end in the puzzle.

Mark was undaunted. He summoned up the professor provocateur from his past. "OK, let's focus! Let's put all the Brauweiler data out of our minds. It's fraudulent, so it never existed. What facts do we know about this monster?"

One by one, the team recited the facts, as Tony patiently took notes. He had been through this drill with Mark before. High fevers, sudden onset, all male patients, were facts that came out first. Symptoms and clinical data were easy, and Tony had a long list.

When they bogged down, Art declared a rest room and refreshment break. Returning refreshed, they began to ask questions that bothered them. Why did a virus that looked like meningitis go exclusively to the brain? Jamal pointed out that the nose was a direct route to the brain.

"Jamal, God bless you!" Mark shouted into the microphone. "I know what it is! Meg and I are saddling up, and we'll be there in less than an hour."

Twelve

Mark felt like a rock star as he and Megan walked into the main CDC Conference Room. Everyone was buzzing about the vexing problem of the *Diablo* virus. Mark said he knew the answer. During the last hour, they hadn't been able to solve the puzzle, and they were demanding an answer. Mark wasn't going to oblige them. He taught with the Socratic Method, asking them questions until they reasoned their way to the answer. Many of his colleagues hated that, and a few had even threatened to strangle him.

Art called on the group to take their seats, while Mark sat on the edge of the platform, prepared to lead them through the exercise.

"What does *Diablo* structurally resemble?" he queried. They all agreed that it looked like meningitis. Next, he repeated the question, "Why is it localized in the brain?"

The group thought Jamal's suggestion, that it was taken in through the nose, was reasonable. Still, they didn't get it.

"What do you put into your nose?" Mark prompted.

Valerie leapt to her feet, "It's a vaccine!" she shouted, "a nasal vaccine!"

Mark was still frowning. "And why does it contain human DNA?" he prompted. There was a long pause.

"Because it was cultured in human fetal cells?" Valerie answered uncertainly.

"Bingo!" Mark said, affirming her theory.

Viral uptake of DNA hadn't been observed in a vaccine. It would be a game changer.

Mark yielded the platform back to Megan. "Art, we've got to start collecting samples," she suggested, "and we've got to do it very quietly! If this misdirection play by Brauweiler is related, we don't want to tip them off."

Art agreed, and they drew up a plan to visit clinics, hospitals, and pharmacies. They would concoct a cover story to make the sampling appear routine.

"I think we should also recheck medical histories to see if they were vaccinated," van den Bergh opined.

"That's a great idea," Jamal agreed, "but that might arouse more suspicion than collecting samples."

They agreed to work discreetly to check the records.

After the sub-groups finished their work, everyone focused on Jamal, who was setting up an unscheduled presentation. He had just received a communication from a Los Angeles clinic. They had placed a *Diablo* patient in a PET machine to observe what was happening in the brain. Jamal put up a slide of a normal brain and the next image showed the brain of the *Diablo* patient.

"I've never seen a color pattern like that!" van den Bergh remarked.

The activity was most intense in the cerebrum, the thinking, and reasoning center.

"Now look at the pattern while the patient is having a delirium episode!" Jamal pointed out.

The limbic region, which is responsible for emotion, lit up brightly. They all stared in awe of the monster that was wreaking this devastation.

"So, what happens to the next patient who needs a PET scan?" van den Bergh asked acidly.

"Nothing!" Jamal responded calmly in his melodic Jamaican tone. "They are keeping the unit in the isolation suite. After they're finished, they'll incinerate it."

Mark almost choked on his orange juice. "You mean they can afford to destroy a million dollar piece of equipment?" he stammered. Evidently, the LA clinic had a big budget.

*****

During the break, Jack Dahlkemper slid up next to Megan at the refreshment table. "So that's what a PET scan of a dark spirit looks like," he remarked.

"Ordinarily, I'd recommend a psychiatrist," she responded, "but with all the crazy events we're encountering, I'm willing to consider it!"

"Just think about it," he suggested, "an innocent defenseless life is snuffed out in the womb. Don't you think that spirit would be angry? Picture it as bad karma."

Mark noticed the serious conversation, and opted to join in. Megan told him about Jack's dark spirit ideas.

"Dahlkemper, I didn't think you were that deep," Mark conceded, "but you might be onto something. In Africa, they call it the Dark Arts. In one of the villages we visited, someone threw a dead chicken under the car of a regional official. Several miles down the road, he had a serious accident."

Megan shuddered. "You guys are creeping me out!" she said as she turned and walked away.

"I never expected you to agree with me professor," Jack said.

"I've seen a lot of mileage since you sat in my class," Mark responded thoughtfully. "On reflection, I think I've been jealous of you. You're highly intelligent, good looking, and have the body of a Greek god. I always felt the need to butt heads with you. Maybe we could do a lot more if we worked together!"

*****

Tony and Jack gave the final presentation of the day. Jack showed a map which highlighted the sites where his team had collected ticks and mosquitoes. Tony displayed the fluorescence spectra of the *Diablo* virus, and a series of spectra from bugs collected from the different sites. It was a nerd's ballet.

As Jack moved the pointer east, from Tennessee into North Carolina, Tony changed the spectrum. As the trek moved, the spectra of the bugs got closer to the *Diablo* spectrum. Tony summed up the bad news, "It appears that structural elements of the virus are showing up in mosquitoes and ticks."

Jack put a positive spin on the results, "Mosquitoes and ticks don't migrate very far. Any spread would be caused by the host."

Tony went off script to get in the last word, "Analysis of the protein showed that the mosquitoes clip off pieces of the coat protein." As soon as he said it, Tony knew he was in trouble.

Mark shifted around in his seat. That was negative body language. For the next hour, Mark ripped Tony's assumptions to pieces.

After the meeting adjourned, Mark surveyed the refreshment table, and selected an ice tea. He glanced back toward the door, and spotted Jim and Mandy engaged in an animated conversation. *Now that's an odd couple,* he thought. Mandy began tenderly to brush Jim's face. Mark knew that signal well.

As the odd couple walked toward the door, Mark commented under his breath, "Don't do it Jim!"

*****

Sandi and Nick were working feverishly on the five maps taped to the living room walls of Nick's condo. It was almost noon, but they were still dressed in their bed clothes. Sandi stretched to draw a line at the top of the map, as Nick mangled the pronunciation of an obscure city in Iceland. The deep pile carpet crept up around her bare feet as she reached higher. The faces of the five maps, each representing a suspicious stock trade, looked like a rogue spider had spun webs across them. Each black line represented trades made at the same time, and the red lines showed an organizational relationship.

"Let's take a break," Nick suggested, realizing they hadn't eaten yet.

Sandi pulled her disposable phone from the pocket of her robe, dialed Joshua's Deli, and ordered two Reuben's. The food critic at the *Examiner* had told her they were in the top five, and they delivered. Nick had retreated to the master bath to shower and freshen up.

Sandi was relieved that he was working from home that day, where she was better able to protect him. She had been afraid to tell Susie that she and Nick had fallen in love. She had fully expected Susie to scream at her, and dreaded that she might replace her, but Susie had been surprisingly calm.

"I've been there myself," she said wistfully. "I was assigned to protect a team of researchers in Georgia, and I fell for the team leader. I didn't act on it, and another blonde scooped him up."

"Who was he?" Sandi had asked curiously.

"You'll see him at the next press conference that Tattler covers on that new virus!" Susie replied mysteriously.

Sandi was jolted out of her reverie by the sharp rap on the door. "Wait a minute!" she called. Quickly, she peeled off the top of her robe, slipped on the underarm holster, and pulled the robe back on. She picked up her work phone to check out the hallway camera. It was a young delivery man. He didn't look like a professional assassin, just a college kid trying to make a few bucks.

Just in case, she checked to make sure she had a clear path from her hand to her weapon. Nothing was one-hundred-percent in her business.

She opened the door, slipped him the thirty dollars, including tip, took the sandwiches, and quickly shut the door. She checked to make sure the bag contained nothing other than sandwiches. At the same time, she kept an eye on the external cameras to make sure the deliveryman was not contacting anyone else.

Nick emerged from the master suite casually dressed. He went to the kitchen, poured two glasses of wine, and placed them on the table. Sandi had laid out the sandwiches, and they began to dine. Sandi noted that the corned beef was so tender that it melted in her mouth. She resolved to thank the food critic for her recommendation.

Moving back to the living room, they resumed making notes on the maps.

"Whoever it was did a helluva good job of hiding the collusion," Nick remarked irritably.

They followed the red lines, and discovered the trails ended at private companies throughout Europe. Nick dialed up Stu to compare notes.

"We're stuck," complained Stu. "Private companies don't have to share their financial data! I'll bet they're laundering the money through the Caribbean."

"It's just going to take a lot of shoe leather Stu," countered Nick.

Sandi was quickly typing the names of the companies into her data buffer. What was needed in this situation was a super spy. She set her encryption to max, and fired off the list to Susie.

Stu updated them on the status of "the kid," now referring to himself as Houdini. Apparently, some unsavory characters were trying to locate him. Houdini was leading them through a hall of mirrors through cyberspace and social media. Sandi was visibly concerned.

"Tell that kid that this is no video game," she warned. "If this is a billion dollar operation, these people are extremely dangerous!"

"Now you have me scared," Stu admitted. "Those guys know where I am."

Sandi and Nick advised him to report it to the *Examiner's* security. They could decide whether to alert Atlanta PD.

*****

In a dilapidated stone building on the outskirts of Paris, a middle-aged Swiss man was monitoring their conversation off the satellite feed. The powerful computer by his side was busily trying to break the encryption.

Thirteen

Megan and Mark stopped to look at the paper taped to the wall of the North Georgia Hospital corridor. It had a good quality drawing of an old couple holding pistols. The caption read, "WANTED – ALIVE." They had heard about these posters, but this was the first one they had actually seen. They were showing up in hospitals across the country. The editorial on the page raged against the Health and Human Services policy that denied care to those patients considered terminal. These impromptu posts usually had a very short life. Security was removing them on sight.

"Thank God you haven't had any incidents here," Megan remarked.

"That's because we're ignoring the directive," retorted Mark, not quite able to hide the anger in his voice. "We're not going to use that Third Reich defense, 'we were only following orders'. At least in Africa, they can say they don't have the resources. Here we have the resources, so there's no excuse!"

Paul Tanner, a day shift security officer, said hello to Mark and Megan, then walked on, ignoring the poster.

*****

Jack Dahlkemper had arrived early for the conference call to the CDC. After greeting Megan and Mark, he related a story about a strange encounter in the North Carolina Smoky Mountains.

"I was checking my bug traps near Centerville yesterday. A weird looking guy approached me on the trail, and started talking about the virus. He kept insisting that it was caused by S-1460."

Mark thought that Jack was going woods crazy. "Who was he?" he asked suspiciously.

Jack sensed Mark's incredulity. "I know, I know, I couldn't believe it either," he admitted. "He wouldn't identify himself, but he had a German accent and he was definitely a gangster."

Mark was even more incredulous. "I assume he didn't tell you that, so how do you know?" he pressed.

"I know gangsters when I meet them," argued Jack. "I played football with guys that had gang connections. Gangsters have similar behaviors that transcend nationality. This guy was making a lot of veiled threats!"

That revelation disturbed Megan. Did that guy know that the CDC was collecting samples? Would she and her children be in danger? Vivid memories of the attempted murder of Sal Bonea during the prion epidemic came rushing back.

A harsh tone announced that the videoconference connection had been established. Art opened the session by introducing Midge Fisher, the head of the sample collection team. To Megan, Midge needed no introduction. Megan had recruited her out of Georgia Tech, and had been supervising her for three years. At the time, she had no idea how valuable Midge's forensic courses would be. Everyone else went through the ritual of introducing themselves.

Midge put the first table up on the data screen, the data from the Western Region, and almost all the big city hospitals and clinics were labeled with asterisks.

"We noticed that reps from Cinavax had gotten there ahead of us, and swapped out their meningitis vaccine for a new lot," she explained. "We had a big hyperactive team, so we beat them to the small and mid-size towns!"

Midge went through the other regions, which had the same mixed results. She had persuaded most of the clinics to share their inventory data. None of the lots were past their expiration date. With the massive volume of data, everyone knew that Cinavax was trying to cover something up.

Art took back the camera and presented the laboratory results. They had all been suspicious, but as this data rolled out, they were agitated into a blind rage. All the samples that had not been replaced exceeded the legal limit for human DNA. One lot contained five-thousand times the maximum allowed. Over half the samples contained viruses which resemble *Diablo*. Art also reported that Paul Peterson had developed a rat model to see if the contaminated samples would cause the disease.

"How could this happen?" demanded Mark. "This is scientific fraud and malpractice!"

Valerie Price signaled for the camera. "Producers use membranes for filtration," she speculated. "If there is a tear in the membrane, or if it's installed poorly, the shear could disrupt the fetal cells and release the DNA. The fact that there are multiple lots indicates that their quality control folks were napping."

When they came to the agenda item for "next steps," everybody was chomping at the bit to participate. It took the combined efforts of Art, Megan, and Mark to quiet the uproar. Art took the lead.

"I'll send an urgent notice to the FDA, wait the respectful fifteen minutes, and then issue a press release. Meg, I need you to handle the press."

They began to debate whether the clean lots of the vaccine could be used safely.

"I think we should stop using fetal cells to culture vaccines," suggested Valerie. This kicked off a vigorous debate from both sides of the abortion issue. "All right, I admit it," Valerie responded. "I was raised in a pro-life Christian home, but I'm talking about risk analysis. Remember, the FDA removed fetal cultures from childhood immunizations because of the correlation with autism!"

Mark was chuckling to himself about this little Vietnamese girl with the Southern accent. Many people didn't take her seriously, at their own peril. She was just so damned brilliant.

*****

Megan kissed her husband and started toward the parking lot. She was rushing to get to the CDC. "Pick you up at 5:30," she called back over her shoulder.

"Don't be late," warned Mark. "Karen is making Yankee pot roast!"

He knew so well, how time slipped away in a crisis. So many thoughts were colliding in his head as he sauntered toward the cafeteria.

The temperature was a perfect seventy-five degrees, as a stiff breeze was blowing the cotton ball clouds across the azure sky. The gentle bubbling of the Chattahoochee River welcomed Jim and Mark back to its banks. They had not taken their post-lunch walk together for almost six months. Mark was in good spirits. He had recuperated from the African intestinal parasites, he was home with his family, and they had solved the mystery of *Diablo*. Jim looked like a forlorn lost puppy. Mark tried to probe for the problem, but Jim was not responding. So, they talked in generalities.

They met Tony and Valerie, returning from their walk with their arms around one another. They did their river stroll before lunch. They paused just long enough to exchange greetings and pleasantries. Jim was finally provoked into conversation.

"Lucky couple!" he remarked; "they're really into each other."

"Jim, they're newlyweds," Mark pointed out. "Let's wait and see what they're like after three or four kids!" They walked along in silence until they reached the boat ramp, their turn-around point.

On the way back, Jim couldn't hold it in any longer. He admitted that he had a sexual encounter with Mandy after the last *Diablo* meeting. He was flying around in an emotional tornado, alternately feeling guilty, and then trying to decide whether he was in love with Mandy.

"Have we reversed roles, and I'm your confessor?" Mark asked incredulously.

"I'm a Baptist," Jim laughed, "we don't go to confession."

Mark searched for the right word. He finally parroted back what Jim had told him, when their situations were reversed. He reminded Jim that God was merciful, and that Jesus had come to free sinners. Jim wanted to know whether he should tell his wife.

"There's that old saying that the truth will set you free," Mark opined. "In my experience, that means if you tell your wife the truth, she will throw you out on your ass!"

Back at the hospital, there was a congregation in front of the big screen in the cafeteria. A breaking news story on the epidemic was playing out with unexpected drama. Art had put out the CDC press release, after alerting the FDA. The FDA response was swift and shocking. The agency refused to recall the vaccine, and only imposed quarantine on the affected lots. The FDA spokesman dismissed the CDC's results as "preliminary." The North Georgia researchers exploded with fury. One man punched a table so hard that several dishes flew onto the floor.

"Why don't they just come out and say we're totally incompetent?" Mark shouted angrily.

"They're afraid of offending the Chinese," Jim replied soberly. All that time reading newspapers had given him good insights.

Mark felt a gentle touch on his arm.

"Mark, I need your help with something," Mandy said softly.

As he followed her to her office, he concluded that she wanted his help to let Jim down gently. She closed the door and described her predicament.

"We have five patients that badly need chemotherapy. The Payment Board is refusing to cover it. I'm almost out of contingency money." It wasn't at all what he had expected.

"Meg and I can pledge five hundred out of our next check," he mumbled.

"Oh, I need a lot more than that from you," she said softly.

Mark began to sweat. They had intimate history and her voice was so seductive.

"I'm meeting with a group of wealthy donors on Friday night," she continued. "I'd like you to come and talk about your sabbatical in Africa. Show them we're all about healing the sick. The media guys are all yours to put together the presentation."

"Of course," he sighed with relief, "It's the least I can do!" She leaned over and kissed him softly on the cheek.

Walking back to his office, he began to wonder what was really going on. Why did the Payment Board impose a death sentence on these people? Were the Feds beginning to figure it out? North Georgia Medical Center was taking patients that other doctors were labeling terminal, and dramatically extending their lives. They couldn't hide their success. It was all in the electronic records.

Then there was Mandy. On the surface, most people just saw a sexy woman with loose morals. A rare few were privileged to see the heart of gold and the hard work. He ducked into the men's room to wash his face. He wasn't about to explain Mandy's lipstick to Megan.

On the drive home, Mark described what Mandy had planned for Friday night. Megan was pleased with the goal, but why did it have to be with Mandy?

Mark explained that Mandy was a genius at raising and managing money. So far, she had been the only one to step up to do it.

"All right," Megan conceded, "as long as you're not planning to sleep with her!"

Mark winced. He suspected that Megan knew about that one night stand, but they had never discussed it before. "You know that you're my *Eros* and my *Phila*," he countered. "That wins out over *Eros* alone every time."

"I love it when you talk theology," she quipped.

Megan described the bedlam at the CDC following the press releases. The scientists who had worked all night to do the DNA tests were talking about an armed invasion of the FDA.

"Art was very low key while he was talking to the reporters," she said. "Later, he went into his office, closed the door, and called Washington. We could hear him yelling all the way to the end of the hall!"

Megan speculated that it was payback for the time that Susie Michaels had bullied the FDA during the prion epidemic.

*****

Karen had outdone herself preparing dinner. She had set up the dining room table in formal fashion, with place mats and napkin holders made by the twins. The good china and silverware were out. They could cut the Yankee pot roast with a fork. Megan and Mark were effusive with their praise.

"It's the least I could do for my favorite newsmakers," Karen responded.

Over the apple pie and coffee, Karen broke the news. She had bought a house in Marietta, and was making plans to move out. She reassured them that she would wait until day care arrangements could be made for the twins.

A lot of hugging and kissing, along with a torrent of tears broke out. It was going to be like losing Mary Poppins.

They put on a movie for the kids, and sat down in the living room to talk about adult matters. Mark and Megan's phones both sounded priority text alerts. Jamal had notified the team that two patients from a Lake Lanier houseboat, both infected with *Diablo* had been admitted to the isolation unit. The devil had come down to Georgia.

Fourteen

The press was rowdy and impatient because the briefing was an hour late.

Thank God this isn't my show! Megan thought, as she gazed through the doorway at the pandemonium.

Security had been overwhelmed, and was inexperienced at clearing press credentials. Mandy looked stressed as she stood by the doorway, directing traffic. Everyone was waiting for Jamal Winston, who was supposed to be the star of this briefing. He had been held up treating the two critical patients in the isolation ward. Mark was shaking hands with Al Jackson; who had just flown in from Washington. It was going to be a neurological dream team.

Jamal arrived with wet, matted hair, just out of the decontamination unit. He had hastily thrown on his lab coat, and didn't notice that he had misaligned the buttons and the holes. Mandy intercepted him and whispered in his ear, which allowed him to make the adjustments. He ascended the podium and introduced himself and the other members of the team. His melodic voice seemed out of place for a discussion of such a grim subject.

"I'd like to welcome Doctor Albert Jackson, my boss and member of the National Academy of Medicine," Jamal said.

He began to describe the status of the two patients admitted with *Diablo*. Both men were in extremely critical condition. The symptoms were high intractable fever and intense hallucinations. In fact, one of the men had broken two restraining straps. Megan felt a shiver course through her body, as she remembered the biblical story of the man possessed by a demon. None had been able to bind him.

After the briefing concluded, the cacophony of questions erupted. Megan was impressed with Jamal's calmness. He took his time, called on a reporter, repeated the question, and calmly formulated a response. He was a natural. He politely refused requests for personal information about the patients. Jamal refused to speculate or comment on any question that someone else could better answer. In the end, the press was dissatisfied, but that was par for the course. Afterwards, the team lined up to congratulate Jamal on his performance.

"Mandy told me everything to do," he said sheepishly.

*****

Megan immediately recognized the strikingly beautiful brunette, washing her hands in the ladies room.

"Aren't you with Nick Polakov?" she inquired.

Sandi turned to face her. "Yes, aren't you married to Doctor Selby?"

"Yes," Megan responded suspiciously, "are you a reporter?"

"No," Sandi laughed softly, "I just help my fiancé. He's just so busy, that it's the only way to spend time together."

Megan nodded. That was a situation she could certainly understand. They began to talk about their men and their careers. Mark and Nick were similar in several ways. They could both assemble scattered facts into a sensible story. Sandi described the Justice Drayton scandal. Megan told about how Mark identified the vaccine as the cause of the epidemic. Suddenly, they realized that they'd been talking for over thirty minutes. They exchanged business cards and agreed to get together for lunch.

As Megan was walking away, Sandi was firing off a text to Susie, "Had a nice chat with your old boyfriend's wife."

*****

Tony, Jack, and Mark were poring over a map of Lake Lanier, when Megan strolled into the lab. "You guys must be plotting something sinister," she concluded.

"Jack is going to trap some bugs for us," Tony replied seriously.

"Where have you been hiding out?" inquired Mark.

"I met Nick Polakov's fiancé in the ladies room, and we had a nice talk," she explained.

"Was she the hot one in the black sun dress?" Tony inquired.

"Easy Romeo," teased Mark, "you're already taken."

Tony blushed and tried to explain that good scientists are observant. Jack and Mark continued to try to embarrass him. Mercifully, Megan tried to herd them back to business.

"We haven't established insect transmission yet," she challenged.

"Jamal and I went over the medical records for these guys," Mark countered, "and they've never been vaccinated for meningitis. They both have mosquito bites all over their bodies."

Megan threw up her hands in exasperation. "Great, we just told the world that Cinavax is the source, and now we have exceptions popping up!"

*****

Valerie Price was frustrated. She had been looking at the surface of *Diablo,* and making measurements for weeks. There were several sites that looked promising for antibodies to attack, but developing a vaccine would be a long-term process. The additional complication was that the virus was produced by a vaccine. The FDA would be a lot tougher on proof of safety. Now she was looking for targetable areas for antiviral drugs, currently approved or close to approval. Nothing in the coat protein looked encouraging.

Megan stuck her head in the door to say hello. When she saw how stressed Valerie was, she came in to see if she could help. Valerie explained the problem. Megan suggested looking at the surface carbohydrates. After examining the data, they decided they needed a supercomputer to get a more accurate structure.

"Tony could get it done for you," suggested Megan.

"I'll ask him when we're in bed," Valerie said, giggling.

The tension relaxed, and they spent a few minutes in casual conversation.

Megan's phone sounded its priority tone. It was her administrator calling to tell her that all hell was breaking loose back at the CDC. The Secretary of HHS had just removed Art Munoz from his position. Two-thirds of the staff had walked out in protest. Megan asked who was replacing Art, and then almost passed out when she heard the answer. It was her old nemesis, Richard Tippet, who had sexually harassed her on a number of occasions.

"If he asks, tell him I'll be working out of North Georgia," she said curtly. She hurried off to do damage control.

A crowd was gathered in front of the screen in the cafeteria. Everyone was asking Megan why this had happened. She shrugged and answered: "That's why I'm standing here with you watching the news." The network reporter read a terse statement from HHS, which cited philosophical differences with other agencies.

"That means the FDA," Megan muttered to the people standing next to her.

The news camera panned over the crowd, marching around the CDC, chanting Art's name. Megan squinted to see who was staring. She saw Paul Peterson, Mary

Costanza, and Midge Fisher. She assumed there were others out there, who were also doing work on the *Diablo* project. She felt a touch on her shoulder.

"Meg, can we go talk in my office?" Mandy asked.

Megan had never seen Mandy's office, and was quite surprised that it was so Spartan. The only item hanging on the wall was a framed poster of Martina McBride. On the bottom, there was artistic lettering of a line from one of her hits. It read, "You can spend your whole life building something from nothing, and one storm can come and wash it all away. Build it anyway." Megan finally got an insight into what Mandy was all about. They sat together on the modest fabric upholstered couch.

"Meg, I'm sorry I didn't approach you first about Friday night," Mandy began. "I hope you can come with Mark."

"I really need to get home to relieve Karen. My kids are going to forget who I am," Megan politely declined.

"I promise I won't keep Mark out too late," promised Mandy.

"Well, I doubt that it's as dangerous as Africa," Megan quipped.

"I'm not so sure," mused Mandy. "There are a few old dinosaurs that can bite pretty hard!"

They finally got around to the subject that most concerned Mandy. "What's going on at CDC, and how serious is it?" she asked.

"HHS canned Art because he defended his people from the slingshots of the FDA," Megan opined. "Tippet is an opportunist and serial sexual harasser. Most of the staff will refuse to work for him!"

Mandy explained her concerns. She was fighting a two-front war. The Payment Board was refusing to pay for chemotherapy for patients over the age of seventy. The hospital was using slush funds to pay for the treatments. Now the patients in the isolation unit were costing a ton of money. Megan saw the look of desperation on Mandy's face, and concluded that the hospital was in financial trouble.

"We need to get a handle on this epidemic," Mandy said, while tears and mascara streaked down her cheeks.

Something inside Megan clicked. It was a mixture of fear, outrage, and determination. She put her arm around Mandy's shoulders, and assured her. "You're not alone. We'll pull together a team of good people. We'll fight this disease, and we'll fight all those bureaucratic bastards! I promise that I'll stand with you."

They moved to Mandy's expansive desk, a gift from her former boss, and began to draw up their list. The base was easy to fill. Doctors, nurses, and scientists were mainline idealists. People with influence were harder to identify. They were often prisoners of politics. Mandy had the attention of more than a few wealthy donors, but would they be willing to help storm the castle? In the midst of their confusion, they almost overlooked one of their own.

"Al Jackson!" they shouted in unison. "He spends so much time in Washington, he must have connections."

Mandy hit the intercom button and asked whether Dr. Jackson was still in the house.

*****

Megan and Mandy rushed into the anteroom of the isolation unit. They spotted Al and Jamal staring at a chart, while a robot adjusted the patient's IV inside the hermetically sealed room. They got Al's attention and asked to see him when he was finished.

Al stepped into Mandy's office and shut the door. He still carried the aroma of the decontamination fluid. He hugged the two women that he hadn't seen for over six months. He was still on staff, but was spending most of his time in Washington.

"Al, are you ready to lead a revolution?" Megan asked.

"I think I already am," noted Al, "the majority of the Academy is on the side of the angels, but we're in a cage match with the politicians!" He observed the confused looks on their faces, and went on to explain. "After the Great Depression, the government set up Social Security. That Trust Fund was a big pile of money that was just too tempting, and politicians started borrowing from it. Now they owe over three trillion, and they can't pay it back. Their only recourse is to encourage old people to die."

Mandy and Megan were stunned. They had heard this from crazy conspiracy theorists, but now it seemed to be true.

Al picked up the pen and pad on the desk. "We've got two independent problems," he pointed out, "and we need to keep them independent. The first is that you're not alone in the revolution. Now, I'm an African-American."

"We never noticed," Megan quipped with a quiet laugh.

"Take my word for it," he chuckled. "I read a lot about the Underground Railroad, and how they carried the slaves to freedom. A small group of us in the National Academy are setting up something similar. We're taking patients, condemned to death by the Payment Board, and transporting them to get treatment."

Mandy looked puzzled. "I never heard anything about it," she blurted out.

"That's because it's top secret!" Al retorted. "Remember, we're going against the government's goal to reduce the elderly population. That makes us enemies of the state!"

"So we're practicing black market medicine?" Megan asked.

"You got it!" exclaimed Al. "We take everything off electronic records for these patients, and go back to paper!"

They turned their attention to the *Diablo* epidemic.

"Meg, do you think CDC's work is going to be affected by this walk-out?" Al inquired.

"Definitely!" Megan replied. "Art Munoz is a popular leader. Tippet is a horse's ass. I don't think he'll get even half the staff to come back."

"Then we'll have to get the essential people here to keep the project moving," Al insisted.

"We have lab space and equipment," said Mandy, "but we're awfully tight on money."

"I might be able to help with that," Al suggested. "I'm having lunch with Susie Michaels next week. Maybe I can talk her out of some Homeland Security money!" He noticed that Megan was giving him a fishy stare. "What?" he shouted. "She takes me to dinner once a month. She thinks I saved Agent Foster's life."

They identified the key people that would be essential right away, Paul Peterson and Mary Costanza needed to complete animal model studies.

"You need to order some XL lab coats for Mary," Megan suggested to Mandy. "She's got enormous boobs."

Midge Fisher would be essential for her forensic background, in case their research uncovered any criminal activity.

By the time they finished, they were all late for scheduled appointments. Mandy threw her arms around Megan and began sobbing. She had been in the dead end of a maze, and now she felt free again. Megan held her firmly, gently stroking her back. It was her day to make new friends.

The text that Megan had been ignoring all afternoon remained unread. Richard Tippet had called a staff meeting for ten a.m. The last line was ominous. "Anyone not attending will be terminated."

Fifteen

Nick and Sandi drove quickly on a figure-eight pattern through the side streets of Buckhead. Earlier, they had thoroughly examined the interior and exterior of Nick's car for tracking devices. They had removed the batteries from their cell phones. They had been stunned by the note from Stu that had been slipped under Nick's door.

It read, "The *Examiner* comm-link has been hacked. Meet me at the picnic area at Stone Mountain ten a.m. tomorrow." The instructions to avoid surveillance had been quite detailed.

"I didn't know Stu was good at this spy stuff," Nick had remarked.

"I thought he was just a nerd bean counter!" Sandi had agreed. As a professional, she couldn't have done any better.

Now they were discovering how enslaved they had become to GPS navigation. They had planned to take the side roads to Stone Mountain, and now they were lost. Nick pulled to the side of the road and checked the map, which they had packed for just this contingency. Finally, they found their way to the highway that led them to the park, arriving twenty-minutes late.

Stu fidgeted at a table near the lake, shaded from the bright sun by a cluster of dogwood trees. A large, blue, and white Igloo cooler sat on the table, providing a credible cover for their meeting.

Stu explained what had happened. A routine security check on the *Examiner* comm-link system had turned up a sneaky little piece of spyware embedded in the operating code making all phones, text messages, and e-mails accessible to the intruder. The vendor insinuated it was probably done by someone inside the newspaper. Until they could sort it out, they had to go back to old-school methods.

Stu pulled a stack of papers from the cooler, and passed them to Sandi and Nick.

"It really looks prettier on paper than it does on a computer screen," Stu commented.

The 3-D graph showed the trading activity of twenty-five firms trading a single stock over a ten-day period. It looked like a random pattern of hills and valleys.

"It's a masterpiece," Stu said admiringly, "like a classic performed by a symphony orchestra."

He went on to explain that there were hundreds of firms buying and shorting stocks, apparently at random. However, when he studied the combined profits and losses, those firms were making tons of money.

"Now compare it to these two stocks," Stu pointed out. "These are like a start-up garage band!"

Nick could see the obvious difference in trading patterns. The names of the two stocks were familiar.

"Aren't these the two companies involved in the epidemic?" Nick asked.

Stu grunted. "Yeah, they were trading around news events, and they got sloppy."

"And you're telling me a high school kid figured this out?" Nick marveled.

The sun had moved to the other side of the table, and was now beating down on them. They all agreed to move to another table in the shade. Now they had the "what" and "when" of the crime; all they had to do was fill in the "who" and "why" of the story. The most promising method might be to focus on the two stocks where the conspirators had been sloppy.

"The pattern on the vaccine company seems a lot worse than the drug company," Nick observed.

"That could mean they had less control of the story about the vaccine maker," Stu suggested.

"I wish we knew the inside details of those two stories," Nick groused.

"I know who does!" Sandi said brightly. She expertly popped the battery back into her cell phone and made the selection from her contact list. "Megan," she said, "this is Sandi. How would you like to meet for lunch on Friday?"

After a few minutes of logistics and small talk, the rendezvous was set. As they were preparing to disband, Stu delivered another shocker.

"I did a preliminary estimate," he said calmly. "For the hundreds of companies we've identified, they're making a profit of twenty-two billion dollars per quarter. That's the minimum and it's only for stocks with the highest Appledorf values. That's just in the U.S."

Nick was visibly shaking with anticipation. "The other question is what are they doing with all that money?"

"Nothing good," Sandi interjected. "They can start wars; take over countries, and loot treasuries."

Sandi left one thought unsaid. They could also kill nosey reporters.

Stu resolved to look more closely at how they were laundering the money.

*****

Nick and Sandi knew that the foreseeable future was going to be a tough slog, filled with hard work and high stress. They decided to take a couple of hours to have fun. Stone Mountain had just refurbished its rides, so they skipped the train and elected to visit the top of the mountain. The view of the surrounding area was incredible. Too bad Sandi was observing the tactical possibilities. What a great spot for a sniper! she thought.

On the stern-wheel river boat, they stood at the railing of the upper deck, and beheld the collage of trees, blue water, and the magnificent mountain in the background. It was like a scene out of a romantic movie. They kissed and held each other tightly.

Nick suggested that they should start planning their wedding. Sandi agreed enthusiastically. Susie owed her at least six weeks of vacation time. The most pressing problem was how to tell Nick why she had burst into his life.

On the way home, they stopped at a small roadside diner for coffee and a bite to eat. Stu hadn't had the foresight to pack any food into the cooler. Sandi excused herself to go freshen up. She locked the door of the small dingy rest room and did a quick bug scan.

Her "Urgent" label patched her call to Susie, who had just stepped out of a meeting. Sandi quickly reported on the main points of the meeting. Susie whistled softly when she heard how much money was being pirated.

"No wonder our economy is dragging its ass on the ground," she remarked.

Sandi expressed her concern about the danger to Nick. "I've got to tell him!" she insisted.

"No!" Susie exploded. "I told you that falling in love would cloud your judgment. What if that starts a fight and he throws you out? That would put him in a lot more danger!"

Sandi conceded the point, and promised that under no circumstances would she reveal her identity to Nick. Love was indeed turning out to be a tender trap. Susie committed to look discretely into the conspiracy.

Traffic was beginning to build for the afternoon rush and Sandi attentively watched each neighboring car as they moved from one traffic light to another. She was relieved when Nick pulled into the garage. She checked the status of the security camera on her cell phone. Everything was normal.

On entering the condo, Nick popped the battery back into his phone. Urgent message alerts began to demand attention. The *Examiner's* editor had called an emergency meeting of the staff for nine a.m. The subject was the security breach of the comm-link, and a report on which files had been compromised. Nick checked the confirmation box, indicating that he would be there.

Sandi adjusted the temperature of the shower. They had worked up a sweat and collected some dust during their exploration of Stone Mountain. She stepped in and selected her Neutrogena moisturizing soap. Nick stepped in beside her, embracing her and nibbling on her ear. They began playfully to soap one another, in a combination grooming ritual and foreplay. They had longed for each other all day and for the first time, they had mad, passionate sex in the shower.

After drying off, they lay on the bed together, holding one another tightly.

"Let's order in," Sandi suggested. They quickly agreed on Chinese. Paul Chan's, three blocks away, had a fabulous Peking duck. Sandi entered the order online, remembering Nick's favorite, vegetables with Thai peanut sauce. Nick wanted to talk about the wedding. He proposed a quick wedding, with a civil ceremony. What a romantic! Sandi thought wryly. She insisted on a one-year engagement and a church wedding. She hadn't been a religious person, but it just seemed that they should make a lifetime commitment in a church. Nick couldn't understand why she wanted to wait for a year.

"We'll know each other much better," she argued. "Besides, once we get married, the honeymoon is over!"

*****

Sandi was jolted into wakefulness by her phone. Susie's text was cryptic. Trades of Synovir seemed to be an attempt by a mysterious network to destroy the company. Cinavax was different. The network owned a controlling interest subordinated to the Chinese government. The conspiring companies seemed to have advance notice of the CDC results and made an enormous profit through short sales. Reports from a few deep-cover operatives implicated a secret group named Artemis.

Nick and Sandi walked to the MARTA station to take an early train. Sandi carefully scanned the passengers and then snuggled into Nick's shoulder until the next stop. Once downtown, they slowly window-shopped on the way to work. The streets were busy as they approached the *Examiner* building.

Suddenly, Sandi's practiced eye spotted concerted motion in the crowd. In one second, she pushed Nick to the ground and stepped in front of him. In another second, she drew her .380 SIG, flipped off the safety, and shot the lead gunman before he could raise his weapon. Blood and tissue spurted from his eye socket, indicating that the frangible round had shredded his brain. Sandi pivoted to the right and exchanged fire with the second shooter. The crowd was screaming in all directions. She staggered backward, as the sledge hammer impact of a bullet slammed into her chest. Through blurring eyes she saw her adversary bleeding out on the ground. Her vision was growing dimmer as blood was draining from her head. She stumbled back to her left and emptied her magazine into the backup shooter. Her pistol dropped to the ground and her legs could no longer support her weight. She collapsed on top of Nick, who was struggling to get to his feet. Her vision grew dimmer as her warm blood soaked into Nick's jacket.

Everything faded to black.

Sixteen

Megan was up early. Since she and one-quarter of the professional staff had been terminated by the CDC, she had been leading the team at the North Georgia Medical Center. The two institutions were embroiled in a financial and legal food fight. The CDC was alleging that North Georgia was pirating confidential material. The Medical Center was alleging tortuous interference in the contracts with the former CDC employees. The situation was a total mess. Meanwhile, they had to solve the mysteries of the *Diablo* virus.

The news crawler monotonously reported morning's events as Megan prepared to sort out her schedule for the day when a news item, posted "Atlanta," caught her attention. She clicked to rewind it and read in disbelief. She leapt to her feet and ran to her bedroom, sobbing hysterically.

"Mark, Mark!" she screamed, waking him from a sound sleep. "That girl Sandi, the reporter's girlfriend, was killed in a gun battle. I was supposed to have lunch with her on Friday!"

He sat up and she flew into his embrace. He held her tight as she vented her grief.

"She was so nice," Megan sobbed. "I was hoping we could be friends!"

Slowly, they walked back out to read the full story. By this time, everyone else had been awakened by the commotion. Karen sequestered the children in her bedroom, and attempted to comfort them. The kids were understandably frightened by their mother's hysterical outburst.

Mark and Megan struggled to understand the convoluted story. Sandi had been in a gun battle with three unidentified men. Four bystanders, including Nick Polakov, had been wounded and hospitalized.

"Why would she have been involved in a gun battle?" questioned Megan. "Her business card only said that she was a security consultant."

"Maybe she was involved with protecting Polakov," Mark reasoned. "He nailed a lot of high profile people, like crooked businessmen and politicians."

Megan protested that she shouldn't have had such a dangerous job, but Mark pointed out that her gun had been fired until it was empty.

"She might have been able to have taken out at least one," he observed.

Messages began to bombard them, like incoming mortar shells.

"*Diablo* calling," Mark commented sourly.

Megan composed herself and resumed planning her day. Mark stopped to play with the twins for half an hour, briefed Karen on the situation, and then headed for the shower. Megan soon followed him.

*****

North Georgia Medical was crowded. The parking lot was full, despite the car pools formed by former CDC employees. Mark parked on the grass, alongside a dozen other vehicles. The hallways were buzzing, and scientists were elbow to elbow in the labs. Mandy caught their attention, and briefed them on the latest developments. The bad news was that federal funding was being delayed, a not very subtle retaliation for the disputes between the CDC and the FDA. However, this was countered by dramatic increases from the State and private groups. Emory and Georgia Tech were offering lab space.

Mark and Megan stopped by the isolation unit to check in with Al Jackson and Jamal Winston, who provided more good news. The two patients were responding to experimental anti-viral drugs.

"I thought that S-1460 was recalled by the FDA," Mark said, as he examined the charts.

"Obviously, they didn't find it all!" Al replied, sporting a sardonic grin.

"You know you're playing with fire," Mark warned. "The Feds are just looking for a reason to throw us all in the can!"

Al set his jaw in a defiant profile. "I answer to a higher law!" he answered angrily.

"We've got your back," Mark assured him.

*****

Paul Peterson and Mary Costanza were visibly upset.

"Did you get the memo?" he asked Megan.

"Which one?" she inquired.

"The one that says we're losing our health insurance!" Paul snapped angrily.

As a power play, the CDC administrators had cancelled the medical insurance for all employees that had been dismissed.

"We'll take it up with Mandy," Mark assured them. "I'm sure she can get you covered through the hospital."

Megan wasn't quite so sure. She knew the hospital was burning through cash at an alarming rate.

Paul and Mary reported that the contaminated vaccine did induce *Diablo* symptoms in male rats. Females were unaffected. Rat to rat transmission was alarmingly high and they had also found that female rats, exposed to the vaccine, could infect male rats.

"They're very efficient carriers," Mary said.

"Maybe we should have called it the women's lib virus," Paul added, making a lame joke.

"I guess you ladies had better start building an enormous sperm bank," Mark quipped.

Everyone chuckled at the black humor, since little else was funny.

The conversation turned to gossip about what was going on at the CDC. Paul and Mary, through their social contacts, reported that morale was terrible. Most who remained, did so because they had to provide for their families.

"Richard has been behaving like a tin-horn dictator," said Mary. "He's not a good leader, so all he can do is bully and threaten. I'll bet half the people are looking for other jobs!"

"Maybe we can help them out," Megan mused, "but right now, we need to focus on stopping this epidemic."

*****

Mark and Megan continued to make their rounds of the research wing of the hospital. They found Fenn van den Bergh sitting at a desk in the hallway, gazing at a computer screen and tapping on a keyboard.

"What horrible things have you done to get exiled out here?" Mark asked.

Fenn shook his head and replied, "Every square foot in the lab is occupied by a critical experiment. I'm just dealing in history."

Mark noted the extension cord and data cable that snaked through the doorway. "Is that safe?" he queried.

"The wireless network has repeatedly crashed from overloads," Fenn explained. "People are plugging into the old coax cable."

"Next we'll be going back to pens and paper," Mark quipped sarcastically.

Fenn told them what he had found in the medical records of reported *Diablo* patients.

"Computerized medical record keeping is the only good thing that came out of that damned health care reform," he opined. "So far, one-hundred-twenty-eight cases were associated with Cinavax. Only eleven are secondary exposure and only two have no obvious cause."

"Paul and Mary found a much higher secondary infection rate in rats," Megan observed.

"That's evidence that man is not a rat," Fenn replied.

"Well, maybe some of them are," quipped Mark. "A low re-transmission rate is good news. We should have Valerie study close contacts, which didn't contract the disease. Maybe there's an immunity factor!"

"Tony and Valerie are up to their ears working on the nanotech delivery package," Megan pointed out. "Let's put Husseini on it, and Valerie can consult."

Mandy intercepted Megan and Mark on their way to Tony's lab. She needed their input on some project logistics, and shepherded them back to her office. "We've got to move some people to satellite labs," she began. "I need you to tell me which scientists we can move, and who needs to stay together."

They spent the rest of the afternoon planning for the transition.

"I have a little more good news," Mandy announced with a broad smile. "Levy, Bryan, and Logan offered to represent us pro bono to take the Feds to court. Apparently, they were outraged at the high-handed treatment of the CDC employees."

"Are they good?" Mark inquired.

"They're huge, and they have a great track record winning cases against governments," Mandy replied.

"What does everyone do in the meantime?" Megan asked. "Court cases can drag on for years!"

Mandy broke out in a big smile. "I'm way ahead of you," she proclaimed. "We formed our own network. The clinic and hospital are providing free care for displaced CDC employees. We also have reciprocal agreements with nine other hospitals!"

"We're both going to kiss you," Megan exclaimed, as they came together in a group hug.

*****

Alain Lemond gazed at the austere facade of the Hochstrosser Bank in Zurich. It was a small institution, but heavily fortified.

"Be alert," he warned his five man security team, "we are going into the lair of the gnomes," he said, making a Harry Potter reference.

Bruno Hauptmann, Steinberg's personal assistant, came forward to meet the entourage. He was flanked by a half dozen of his own security people. Alain had done his due diligence on Steinberg's organization. Hauptmann had a Stanford M.B.A., but Alain knew that he was also a brutal enforcer. Hauptmann led Alain down the dim Spartan corridor, and into Steinberg's personal office.

The walls of the office were a flat gray, and sparsely decorated with a few family photos. It was a vivid illustration of the Calvinist philosophy of business in Switzerland. The wizened old man did not rise to greet him, nor did he extend his hand. It was a gesture of contempt. Alain was not surprised. He had been briefed by his grandfather, that this was not going to be a cordial meeting.

The old man got right to the point. "You owe us two-hundred-twenty billion Euros, the price of your incompetence."

Alain's face flushed, as he struggled to conceal his anger. The ungrateful old bastard, he thought, as he ticked off in his mind the billions he had made for the old goat.

"I disagree with your characterization," Alain stated calmly. "You were paid your full share of all the money we made on Synovir and Cinavax."

"But you did severe damage to our future potential earnings," Steinberg retorted. "Besides, your incompetent surveillance resulted in a failure to eliminate a grave threat to our anonymity!"

"I hope you are not blaming me for that," Alain said flatly. "After all, it was three of your people who couldn't even handle one little girl!"

Now Steinberg's face flushed with anger. "You will pay us one hundred million Euros, and you will clean up your own mess!" he shouted.

Alain smiled sardonically. "Very well. If you wish, you can have your pocket change, and we will handle the situation. But, as a result, you will forfeit the opportunity to participate in future endeavors."

The old man unleashed a torrent of curses in German and ordered Alain out of his office.

*****

As he entered, Alain noted that Hauptmann's office was well lit and tastefully decorated.

"Is that an original Monet?" he asked.

"Of course," Hauptmann replied proudly.

Alain also noted an Andy Warhol painting on the opposite wall. Hauptmann was obviously a new generation Swiss banker.

"You know that woman was a trained CIA agent!" Hauptmann asserted.

"I know it was three to one, we had the element of surprise, and she was a girl," Alain responded acidly. Hauptmann stiffened in his chair. "I also know that we were deceived by our surveillance team," Alain continued in a softer tone. "They won't survive to deceive us again."

Together they arranged a transfer of operations.

As they walked back through the austere hallway, Hauptmann warned softly, "You know that Herr Steinberg will take this to the Council."

"I'm not at all concerned," Alain replied shrugging. "I have the more cogent argument. Besides, I'm sure the Council will happily divide up your share of the future income."

Alain rejoined his security force, hopped in the stretch limo, and proceeded to the airport.

Seventeen

Nick winced at the stabbing pain in his shoulder, as he tried to bury his face in his hands. The sling on his arm and the pain killers provided only marginal relief. He had been crying almost non-stop since the melee. Susie stood by with one hand on his good shoulder, and the other holding the portable scanner to her ear. She was listening to the encrypted channel, waiting for reports from her team.

Susie had been stunned when she received the call from the Atlanta PD. When she had assigned Sandi to protective duty, she never expected a three-man, killing crew. What had Nick uncovered? Even more impressive, was the fact Sandi had taken out all three shooters.

Susie commandeered a jet and flew to Atlanta in near-record time. She rushed to Grady Hospital behind a police escort. Interviewing Nick took some time. He was overcome with grief, and a little doped up from the pain meds. He was on the ground during the attack, but tried to get up twice to help Sandi and sustained a gunshot wound.

Susie had been disturbed by the complete lack of information from her intelligence agencies. Were they all asleep at the switch, or were they totally incompetent? Her thoughts rushed to whom she could trust going forward. She had picked up the encrypted phone, and dialed the one person she knew had her back.

"Foster," she barked. "This is Michaels. I need your help. Who can you send?"

Foster pondered a minute as he sized up the situation. "I can give you Vitale," he offered. "He's close to retirement, and he claims he's lost a step, but I don't believe it for a second!"

She quickly agreed and they picked a few others to fill out the team.

Susie returned to Nick's room, and spoke briefly to one of the police officers guarding the door before going in.

"Your brother reporters are a pain in the ass!" she complained to Nick, as she approached his bed. "They want to see you at the next press briefing. Are you up for it?"

After considering it, he reluctantly agreed. "I just want to tell everyone how wonderful she was," he sobbed.

Susie had never seen a man cry so much. *It must be great to be loved that much,* she thought.

*****

The press assembled in the Grady auditorium for the six P.M. briefing. The Atlanta Police Chief and the Atlanta

FBI office gave an update on the investigation. There was nothing new to report. Sandi Meyerson was the only identified fatality. DNA was pending on the three gunmen. The police chief introduced Nick to say a few words, and the crowd erupted with frenetic applause and cheers. Reporters were a competitive breed, but when one of their own suffered, they all rallied to his cause. Nick was overwhelmed with the outpouring of support, and stood silent for a few minutes.

He started simply by describing Sandi and how much he loved her. His voice broke a few times as he described how she had stepped in front of him and saved his life. Susie scanned the crowd and noticed that even the tough guys had tears in their eyes.

Afterwards, Susie patted his arm and escorted him back toward his room. Foster approached and whispered in her ear.

Susie turned back to Nick, "Are you ready to see Sandi?"

He choked back the tears again and reluctantly nodded. When they got to the morgue, he was surprised that it didn't look like a dungeon. Susie led him into an adjoining room, where Sandi lay on a gurney. She was so beautiful, that he deluded himself into thinking she was breathing.

"You look pretty damn good for a corpse," Susie exclaimed.

Sandi opened her big dark eyes and smiled weakly. Nick rushed to embrace her, but Susie restrained him.

"Easy cowboy," she warned, "she still has a helluva hole in her chest!"

Nick's joy turned to anger as he confronted Susie. "Dammit, why didn't you tell me?" he demanded.

"The men who tried to kill you were professionals," Susie replied calmly. "Their bosses were probably watching. We'd like them to reveal themselves."

"Then I suppose that you're not her sister either," he reasoned.

"Not biologically," she quipped. "All of my direct reports have their sister Susie as their next of kin."

Nick pulled a chair next to the gurney and he held Sandi's arm firmly and poured out his emotions. She ran her fingers over the sling.

"What happened here?"

"According to our ballistics expert, he caught a ricochet off the pavement that fractured his shoulder," Susie interjected. "By the way, the DNA came up empty for the shooters!"

Sandi glared intently at Susie. "Bullshit," she shot back, "it was an inside job."

Susie stared back at her, "Nick, could you step outside with Agent Foster? I need a few minutes alone with Sandi."

Nick shook his head and stood protectively over Sandi. As far as he was concerned, he never wanted to leave her side again. Sandi gazed up at him lovingly, and nodded, indicating it was okay for him to step out.

Alone in the room, Susie stared at her protégé and asked, "All right, what did you see?"

Sandi shifted her body a little closer wincing from the pain it caused. "The lead shooter was Ricky Cordero," she said in a weak voice. "We trained together at Quantico. In fact, he beat me out as top marksman. The CIA grabbed him up for special ops. They've got to have his prints and DNA!"

"If he was better, how did you get all three of them?" Susie asked, dubious.

Sandi struggled to keep her throat clear. "They had crappy intel," she grasped. "Cordero was surprised to see me, and he hesitated for a second. It let me get him with a single head shot. The second guy had to start firing from a bad angle. I'm surprised he managed to hit me. The third guy got bumped around by the crowd and was late getting into position. Even though I couldn't see straight, it was an easy shot."

Susie patted her gently on the arm and wondered whether love had been the edge on that awful day. She went to the door and let Nick back into the room. A tall thin doctor also hastily entered.

"This is Doctor Hartman," Susie said to Nick. "He's helped us fake a few deaths in the past. In addition, he's a damn fine thoracic surgeon."

Nick's curiosity was piqued. "How did you pull that off in a room full of people, Doctor?"

"It's not as tough as it sounds," he replied with a shy smile. "I'm in charge, and I keep people running and distracted. The sensors are trained to go crazy on a voice tone. I do a faux resuscitation and then the sensors flatline. The clincher is that whenever my patients die, I personally wheel them to the morgue."

Hartman ordered everyone out so he could examine Sandi.

"It's always refreshing to find a doctor who makes morgue calls," Susie quipped.

*****

Susie and Foster moved down the hall to talk, leaving Nick to pace nervously. Susie related Sandi's account of the battle. Foster agreed that it was troubling that no forensic match was found for Cordero in the federal database.

"Could Sandi have been mistaken about Cordero?' Foster suggested. "I don't think so," Susie replied.

"They trained together, and her memory lines up perfectly with Fields's ballistics report."

The two other possibilities were also truly disturbing. Either the intelligence agencies were staffed by incompetents, or this was a conspiracy at the highest levels of the United States Government.

"Could you double check the prints and DNA?" Susie requested. "You're the Deputy Director. They'll share more with you than with the Atlanta PD. Don't mention Cordero. We don't want to tip our hand, just in case the worst case is true."

Foster nodded in agreement.

Hartman emerged from the room and paused to talk to them. "We can probably let her out in a few days, if you have a safe place to keep her."

"We'll protect her," Susie asserted. "At least you won't have to worry about discharge papers. She's officially dead!"

Nick and Susie returned to the room to share the good news with Sandi. The fake funeral would be held in two days. After that, they would slip her out of the hospital and into a safe house.

"Who's in the casket?" Sandi asked curiously.

"An unclaimed body of a woman with no friends or family," Susie replied

Sandi shook her head. "At least she'll have a nice funeral."

Susie excused herself to make the arrangements. As she walked out the door, a messenger handed her a piece of paper. She glanced at it, and her face contorted into a grim smile.

"Hey Vitale!" she called out to the agent down the hall, "want to take a ride with me?"

"Sure thing boss," he boomed. "Where do you want to go?"

"Let's go arrest a snoop team!" she replied acidly.

Susie had gotten to be an expert at slipping in and out of the hospital. Reporters were camping out in the hospital lobby, trying to ferret out the back-story. They would wonder why the National Security Director was hanging around the hospital. Susie had found a fire door, and had bypassed the alarm. She and Vitale sneaked out to find themselves staring at a dumpster.

"How far away is your car?" Vitale inquired, his head on a swivel.

"About three blocks," she laughed.

*****

Traffic on I-75 was backing up in a prelude to rush hour. Susie punched the address into the GPS which directed her to exit at Tenth Street and then onto Spring.

"There's the Varsity," observed Vitale. "I love their food. I put on five pounds the last time I was assigned here."

"Maybe we can stop after we get these guys booked," Susie suggested.

"How many of us are in on this operation?" he asked.

Susie smiled at him, "Just you and me big guy."

"No offense boss," he objected, "but isn't this way below your pay grade?"

"It's personal for me when one of my people gets shot. Don't worry, whatever you need is in the trunk: vests, assault rifles, shotguns."

They pulled onto a side street, and then into the parking lot that Sandi had used as a surveillance base. They opened the trunk, vested up, and selected their weapons. Susie chose a Glock 17, while Vitale opted for a .44 magnum. Susie alerted him that they were loaded with hollow point ammo.

"At least we can minimize collateral carnage in adjacent apartments," she remarked.

The hallways of the apartment building were dirty, dimly lit, and smelled moldy. Vitale led the way up the stairs and up to the door of the apartment. There was no sound coming from inside and no response to Vitale's knock. They drew their weapons as he kicked in the door. The apartment was empty, but it was clear that a violent episode had taken place. Furniture was overturned, glasses and bottles were strewn everywhere, and there were multiple blood stains on the rug. After clearing all the rooms and closets, Susie punched a speed dial button on her phone.

"Fields," she said, "we need your CI team. I'm texting the address."

Susie and Vitale canvassed the adjacent apartments. The neighbors reported that the three men that lived in the apartment were rude, noisy, and inconsiderate. The little gray-haired African-American lady across the hall revealed that there was a lot of shouting the previous night. Then it sounded like they were moving furniture out of the building.

"Did you look out in the hallway or outside?" Susie asked.

"No honey," she replied softly, "they's big bad men. I didn't want no trouble!"

They surveyed the outside of the building.

"I don't see anything around here that looks like a camera," Vitale remarked.

"I think I might know where to find one," Susie mused. They returned to the parking lot across the street. "Want to climb up to the roof with me, Vitale?" Susie asked, laughing.

Vitale was surprised, but he followed her as she pulled herself up onto the fire escape.

"Thank God I'm not wearing a dress," she sighed.

When they reached the roof, they walked to the front of the building.

Susie bent down and retrieved Sandi's AV recorder.

Eighteen

Megan woke with a startle and heard the banging of something against the house. Sinister shadows raced back and forth across the ceiling. The last few weeks had been very upsetting. Jack Dahlkemper had been insisting that the hallucinations, experienced by *Diablo* patients, were caused by angry spirits. Megan was having ongoing nightmares, with angry babies who had been aborted and ground up to supply cells for vaccines. As consciousness pushed out sleep, she realized that it was a loose shutter banging in the wind. Blowing branches illuminated by the outdoor security light, cast the shadows. Now, she could only rationalize the dreams.

Jack was a powerful storyteller. He told graphic tales of voodoo and Santeria rituals and the calamities that flowed from them. As a clinching argument, he cited Professor Gordon Winthrop of King's College. The professor hypothesized that an undiscovered energy, which he called "organizing energy," controlled the other forms of energy and matter. Winthrop's equations were extremely complex, but the phenomena they addressed were easy to understand. For example, why don't the electrons fall into the nucleus of an atom?

"Only a few dozen people in the world understand it," Jack had admitted, "and only four or five believe it could be valid. He's describing something that hasn't yet been discovered!"

Megan brooded briefly, and then concluded that understanding was not going to come into a dark bedroom.

Closer to home, other enigmas nagged at her. The CDC and HHS had agreed to binding arbitration, and then when the arbitrator ruled that Art Munoz should be reinstated, the government reneged. The press pilloried the government, and the professional employees refused to return to work. North Georgia Medical Center won their rights to Medicare compensation in federal court, but the action was now tied up in the appeals process. The future seemed to be enveloped in a very thick fog. Megan stretched and got up to make breakfast for the family and pack lunches.

Mark stumbled into the kitchen looking exhausted. He had been working ten-hour days and then cruising fund-raisers with Mandy in the evenings. Megan threw her arms around his neck and kissed him passionately, just as she had done every day since he had returned from Africa.

"Hey big guy, make any money last night?" she purred.

"Mandy always gets more than I do," he admitted sheepishly. "She works the men and I work the women. I feel dirty, but we need the money pretty damn badly!"

Megan understood. Paying the CDC scientists was putting an enormous strain on North Georgia's budget. "Well, at least you're keeping Mandy away from Jim," she conceded.

Mark shook his head. "He's making way more of this relationship than she is," he said mournfully. "She's not a bad person. She just doesn't have the time to form deep relationships."

Megan played the car color game with the twins, as Mark battled the traffic on the highway to the daycare center. It had been a traumatic experience for the kids and they missed Aunt Karen terribly. Megan felt acute pangs of guilt, and tried to make up for it by packing special treats in the toddlers' lunches. Maybe she had sent signals to Karen that she was jealous, or, maybe Karen was still in love with Mark and living in the same house was too stressful. Of course, Mark was oblivious to the whole situation. He had no problem with two beautiful women catering to him.

*****

Mark and Megan arrived early, but the hospital was already in a state of controlled chaos. They made their way to the auditorium, where Al Jackson and Jamal Winston were presenting a case study on the two latest *Diablo* victims. Mark grabbed two seats in the third row. It was going to be an overflow crowd. Scientists were coming from all over the Southeast to review the latest clinical data.

"G'day mate," a voice from the row behind him said.

Mark spun around to stare at the thin, well-tanned man in the faded jeans. "Jameson, how the hell are you?" he boomed. "Did you come all the way from New Zealand to check out this conference?"

"Mostly I came to see Mary," he said sheepishly. "You blokes are keeping her too busy to come and see me. Looks like you lost a bit of weight in the Congo mate!"

"I'm surprised my exploits are known in New Zealand," Mark said, surprised.

"You're all over the net," Jameson exclaimed. "Blokes and Sheila's are signing up by the hundreds to go there!"

It was obvious to Mark that Father Mukana was skilled in PR. Forgetting for a moment that Karen had moved out, Mark invited Jameson and Mary over for dinner. The Aussie respectfully declined, citing a prior commitment. Mark nodded his understanding. It was obvious that Jameson was looking forward to some one-on-one time with Mary.

As predicted, the auditorium filled to overflowing. Mandy stood in a corner, smiling at the success of the institution. Doctor Gilbert had given her an approving nod. She had come a long way from entry level secretary and in a relatively short period of time. Three factors had pushed her to the top. Certainly, her own work ethic and drive for higher education were essential. Doctor Cullen Davis, the founder of North Georgia Medical Center, had mentored her. Successfully managing through a serious crisis can also demonstrate a person's competence. Mandy had worked day and night to handle the financial administration and funding of the prion epidemic. Since most of the money was from national security sources, she had to handle the administration herself. Now, at the pinnacle of her career, she watched the overcrowded auditorium and hoped the fire marshal wouldn't show up.

Al Jackson took the podium, quieted everyone down, and made a few introductory remarks. Then he turned the presentation over to Jamal, his protégé. Jamal laid out the course of clinical diagnosis and treatment for his two patients, from admission to their deaths. The men had been treated with Synovir-1460, which slowed the progress of the infection. Based on animal models, they added methotrexate as a second drug, but it was too late. Jamal called up Sal Monea to summarize the autopsy findings. The cause of death of both patients was cardiac arrest. Other case histories from around the country cited multiple organ failure. Sections of the brains of the two men showed less deterioration than all comparable cases. Everyone opined that this would indicate that the treatment was beginning to work.

Jamal took back the podium, and indicated that future patients would be treated with a combination of S-1460 and methotrexate. The room exploded with questions and criticisms. Mandy cringed in her corner. She had alerted Al and Jamal that NIH and FDA people had sent in RSVP's. She had provided photos, so Al and Jamal could recognize them but even she hadn't expected this firestorm.

The Head of FDA Compliance accused Al, Jamal and the hospital of malpractice. This was too much for

Al. He leaped to his feet and counterattacked the tormenter.

"This is an epidemic that has no cure. This combination of drugs is the best we have. Sid, you're a regulator, so you care about the rules. We're doctors, and all we care about is saving lives. We don't have time for a seven-year crossover study."

Physicians in the room exploded with cheers and applause, to the astonishment of the government employees.

"Fenn, what do you think?" inquired the Dean of the Tulane Medical School.

Fenn stroked his chin for a few seconds, and then replied, "Al is right! Without this treatment, death is inevitable. We need to try it, and improve it along the way!"

The cheers erupted again and, for the moment, the matter was settled.

*****

The presenters were almost giddy from their success. There was a lot of back slapping and congratulations from physicians in the audience.

"Sometimes we forget to look at patients as people, not sterile statistics," expounded Ralph Dannely, past head of the CDC. "I'm so grateful to Al for reminding us that we are in this profession to heal people!"

Valerie and Tony were chatting with colleagues from Vanderbilt about targeted therapies for the two-drug regimen. The future was beginning to look a lot brighter.

Megan slipped out to use the ladies room which was empty. She had beaten the post-meeting rush. She washed her hands, checked her makeup, and left to return to the auditorium. She was met at the door by a security guard.

"Miss Selby," he drawled, "there's a limo waiting for you out front."

"I didn't order a limo," she protested. "I never ordered a limo."

Curiosity overwhelmed her, as she walked to the lobby with the guard. A long, black limo with shaded out windows was idling at the curb.

"This has got to be a mistake," she insisted.

"No ma'am," replied the guard, "the driver asked me to find Megan Selby!"

She concluded that it must have been some juvenile prank and walked out to explain to the driver. The back door swung open.

"Megan, hop in and let's take a ride," Susie Michaels said.

Susie slid over and Megan climbed hesitantly into the back seat. She recognized Dom Vitale behind the wheel. He waved to her and pulled away from the curb.

"Power down your phone and remove the battery," Susie ordered. Megan fumbled with it, but finally got the battery out. The brunette, wearing sunglasses and sitting on the other side of Susie, looked vaguely familiar.

"Hi Megan," Sandi said, "Sorry we didn't get to have lunch together."

Megan's jaw dropped open and she almost climbed over Susie to get a better look. "You're not dead!" she stammered. "But I was at your funeral!"

"Susie wouldn't let me go," Sandi giggled. "I heard it was very sad."

"Does Nick know?" Megan inquired.

"Nick knows, along with those of us in this car," Susie answered. "She's going to stay dead at least until she recovers. This is top secret, same as our last project. You can tell Mark, but nobody else!"

Susie quickly got into the reason for this ambush meeting. "We're working on a major financial fraud case," she began. "Nick uncovered it, and I assigned Sandi to protect him, after we picked up some chatter. Two companies are involved in your epidemic. Can you give us the whole story?"

Megan told them everything she knew about *Diablo*, while Vitale drove them through North Georgia mountain roads. Sandi and Susie got very interested when she told them about the fraudulent data in the Brauweiler paper, the Chinese vaccine, and the big fights with the FDA and HHS.

"The bastards knew it was the vaccine, but they put out this phony story so they could short the stock," Susie opined.

"I've never understood the stock market," Megan said.

"Don't worry about it," Sandi said, patting Megan on the arm, "we needed a high school kid to figure it out!"

After a few hours of discussion, they pulled back up to the hospital. Megan turned to Sandi.

"Can we get together for lunch now?"

"Dead people don't eat," Susie quipped. "Also, tell Mark not to shoot any of my people. We're going to be checking the security around your place."

Megan smiled, jumped out of the limo, and entered the building. As she navigated the halls, she ran into Paul Peterson.

"Did you hear the news?" he asked. "All of us got reinstated by the Court, even Art! It's been a great day!"

You'll never know how great, Megan thought.

As the limo drove away, Sandi and Susie analyzed the case. "With all that resistance from the FDA and HHS, someone there has got to be involved," Sandi speculated.

"It's worse than that," Susie said glumly. "The CIA says they have no idea who the gunmen were. Jenkins told me that himself. This conspiracy goes all the way to the top!"

Nineteen

Nick woke up at 4:30 A.M. He was having trouble sleeping in the strange bed in the safe house. Also, since the shooting, he hovered over his beautiful lady. She had taken a bullet meant for him, and he was determined that it would never happen again. The old house, where Susie had stashed them, made a variety of creaking, banging, and scraping sounds. Nick constantly imagined that someone was breaking in to kill them.

Slowly and quietly, he eased himself out of bed, hoping he wouldn't wake Sandi. She had been working like a woman possessed, determined to hunt down the fiends that had tried to execute them. Three days ago, she began to run a fever. Vitale snuck her back into Grady, where Hartman treated her for a wound infection.

"Did that bastard rub garlic on the bullet?" she had asked.

Hartman had smiled and reassured her. "That's just an urban legend. Any cultured botulinum would have been defrayed by the heat of combustion. The bullet just carried bacteria from your skin and clothing into the wound."

The powerful antibiotics he gave her made short work of the infection, but Nick insisted that she get more rest.

The high-tech coffee maker was fully charged, so all he had to do was push the button. He glanced at the surveillance monitor, and saw what looked like normal activity in the lower middle-class neighborhood and he knew that Susie's select team was next door watching the same monitors.

Nick poured his coffee and settled into his recliner. The comm-link responded to his touch, but responded with an error message.

"Dammit!" he said softly, "these guys are screwing up my career!"

The whiz kids had modified his communicator to appear to transmit from his condo. Unfortunately, it also caused glitches in linking up.

Sandi appeared from the bedroom, rubbing the sleep from her eyes. She looked stunning in the short negligée, even with her shorter hair and the corner of the bandage showing below her cleavage. Nick could hardly bear the guilt of seeing that wound. He wanted revenge.

"I heard you arguing with someone," she yawned. "Susie's guys screwed up my comm-link," he complained angrily.

Sandi took the device from him and began troubleshooting. After about thirty minutes, she concluded that the problem was on the newspaper's router and not in the comm-link.

"I would say that your paper has been hacked, and all your data has been deleted!" she announced.

He grabbed the comm-link out of her hand and checked his data cache. "They've even deleted it from my link all right," he muttered in disbelief. "How am I going to write a story without any evidence?"

"I have it all," Sandi said quietly. "I've been copying your data since I moved in."

"I don't know whether to strangle you, or kiss you!" he shouted.

"I recommend the latter," she said smiling.

Sandi and Nick worked feverishly to organize the copied information. Before they realized, it was late afternoon, and they hadn't eaten all day. There was a sharp rap on the door.

"I knew they wouldn't let us starve," Nick joked.

Sandi had packed her pistol, out of an abundance of caution. They checked the door monitor and were amazed to see a stern-faced Susie. She rushed in as they opened the door.

"Give me all your cell phones and the comm-link," she demanded. "Take these communicators and pack up. We're moving."

Nick and Sandi shook their heads and demanded an explanation. "I've been fired," she snapped, "and all our lives may be in danger!"

"Did they fire me too?" Sandi asked, as they rushed to pack.

"They couldn't fire you," Susie replied, laughing. "You're dead, remember?"

Vitale and three other agents helped them load up a large, old passenger van.

"As of now, we're an independent army of seven!" announced Susie.

*****

Traffic was light on the side street in the "Pest" section of Budapest. A disguised Claude Lemond, along with two bodyguards, entered the small coffee shop. The proprietor ushered them into the back room. "My bankers," he announced to the waitress and his patrons.

At a table, with two other bodyguards, sat Alain Lemond. "Good afternoon Grosspere," he said respectfully.

"What impetuous thing have you done?" the old man asked scornfully.

"I believe Signor Borghese called it going to the mattresses," answered the young man flippantly.

Claude sat down to hear what he expected would be a fascinating explanation. "You're on the Council a few months, and you turn it upside down!" the old man thundered.

"It was something that had to be done," said Alain defensively. "Steinberg was stuck in the last century. We can't make money with a negative attitude."

Claude was stunned to realize that he had said the same things when he was young.

They took a break away from the others to share a bottle of wine.

"What reaction have you gotten?" asked Alain.

"I had only two members scream at me," answered his grandfather.

"I have the full allegiance of five," Alain retaliated. "One of them is the reason we are meeting in Budapest!"

"So Menyhart is on board?" the old man asked admiringly. To his amazement, one of the secret members supported the plot to purge Steinberg. "So, how did you pull it off?" Claude asked curiously.

"It was easy," Alain bragged. "Herr Hauptmann was easy to convince. He has modern ideas about the future of Swiss banking. He convinced Menyhart."

The deed was done. As soon as all the sore losers were mopped up, the action would be unanimously approved by the Council. They turned the discussion to the situation in the United States.

"We cleared out all the troublemakers from the Administration," Alain boasted, "and we've purged all the files from the CIA and FBI."

"What did you have to promise the President?" Claude wanted to know.

"Only to get her re-elected," Alain said with a shrug. "Electronic voting is a wonderful thing. We no longer have to bus in people with phony ID's. All it takes is a few lines of code. Now the heads of the CIA and FBI were different. They cost us real money!"

"What about the meningitis epidemic?" Claude questioned.

Alain shrugged. "The American doctors are learning how to treat it," he said. "All our money is out. We can just pin the blame on the Chinese."

Grandfather and grandson opened another bottle of wine, leaned back, and reviewed the situation in the rest of the world.

"Nigeria has the rebels in full retreat, thanks to our loans," Claude reported.

"What leverage do we have to assure they pay us back?" inquired Alain.

"It's reversible," said Claude with a broad smile. "Ajax sold them junk weapons, aircraft, and vehicles. Within a year, they'll need a lot of spare parts. Now, what do you have for the elections in the Ukraine?"

Alain stroked his chin and mused, "Lysenko has made us the best offer. We'll use MINOTAUR, our simplified election control code. It will be an opportunity to test it, before we use it on the rest of the world."

They laughed, got up, hugged, and prepared to go their separate ways.

*****

The *Diablo* team stood behind the observation glass in the isolation unit, and watched Jamal conversing with the thirty-five-year-old patient. Just forty-eight hours earlier, the young man had been admitted with a one-hundred-six-degree fever and violent hallucinations. Although he was weak from his ordeal, the man was now lucid and had no apparent brain damage. He did recall the hallucinations in vivid detail, though. The patient was convinced that evil spirits were trying to kill him. Jack Dahlkemper nudged Megan's arm, smiling at how close it came to his earlier predictions.

The isolation ER team had quickly administered S-1460 and methotrexate, as soon as the patient had arrived. A booster dose of S-1460 contained in a folate -

targeting particle was given later. Valerie and Tony had developed the drug targeting strategy, and Synovir was anxious to acquire the rights. The couple agreed to let Mandy negotiate for them.

"At the end of the day, Tony and Valerie will own that company," Megan predicted.

The only residual problem was the patient's reluctance to sleep. He was afraid the dark spirits would return and finish the job.

Mandy gathered the team into the conference room for a celebration. "That's one," she called out as she raised a glass to toast their success. "We're going to perfect this course of treatment, and we're going to celebrate every time we save a patient."

Etienne Gilbert came in and congratulated everyone. "I've been getting offers to run some of the most prestigious hospitals in France," he told them. "They think I did this. I told them I would only consider it if I could bring my entire staff, and my Chief Administrator."

Mandy blushed in a rare display of embarrassment.

"I'll feel a lot better when we can discharge this patient," Al confided to Mark and Jamal.

Twenty

The champagne was flowing in the auditorium of the North Georgia Medical Center. A banner with a large "24-2" was stretched across the front wall, representing their record against the *Diablo* virus. Their treatment was continuing to improve, as they learned more from each new patient. Hospitals from around the world were burning up their phones and website, requesting consultations. Many nearby hospitals were transferring patients to them. Mandy and Art were uncomfortable with this process, since immediate treatment was critical. Together, they worked out a coaching and medication distribution, so patients could receive treatment at their own hospitals.

One remaining aggravation was the FDA. The bureaucracy was resisting going to clinical trials for Valerie's targeted therapy and they were also reluctant to ban vaccines that were cultured with human fetal tissue. Their decision on the second item was becoming irrelevant, however, thanks to wide press coverage, patients and doctors were questioning the origin of all vaccines. Vaccine makers insisted their products were safe, but it didn't matter. Vaccine sales dropped eighty-five percent, and public health authorities went into panic mode. Researchers rushed to develop new culture media. Cinavax, whose stock was wiped out by coordinated short selling, declared bankruptcy. It was an embarrassment to China, whose government leaders were heavily invested in the company.

A rousing cheer exploded, as Jamal walked into the party, after coming off a twelve-hour shift. Mandy hastily took the podium to start the program, since the Governor of Georgia had been waiting patiently to present commendations to the *Diablo* team. He kept his speech short, partly to preserve the festive mood and partly because he was late for another event. He presented special awards to Fenn, Art, and Jamal for leading the clinical team. Mandy congratulated everyone and announced the bar was open again.

Megan might have been celebrating on the outside, but troubling thoughts were racing through her mind. A young nurse had approached her this morning with a disturbing story. She had been monitoring a recently admitted *Diablo* patient on the night shift and saw a dark, shadowy figure emerging from the man. It turned, hissed at her, and walked through the wall.

"Meg, I'm afraid to tell my supervisor," she said in a trembling voice. "She'll think I'm going nuts, and I'm not sure I'd disagree with her!"

Megan was skeptical. "Have you been talking with Jack Dahlkemper?" she inquired.

"No" she said wide-eyed. "I've seen him around and he's hot, but I haven't worked up the nerve to talk to him yet!"

The question burned in Megan's mind. Was there an evil force at work, or was the young nurse cracking under stress?

*****

Claude and Alain Lemond lounged on the sofa in their vineyard mansion. A special closed-circuit feed was displaying election results from the Ukraine. The pro-Russian candidate, who had been trailing in pre-election polls, was building a comfortable lead. Supporters of the nationalist candidate were claiming fraud, but they couldn't point to any evidence.

The Lemond's opened the champagne and lit up their Cuban victory cigars. The election had, indeed, been fixed.

"Romanov did a good job getting that software contract," Alain noted proudly.

"Too bad he made such a mess trying to recruit Ms. Michaels to our side," Claude countered.

His grandson bristled defensively. "I didn't know that he had her thrown into one of Saddam's prisons," he snapped. "If I had known, I'd have sent someone else!"

They switched the huge monitor to computer mode, and brought up the futures currency trades. Their attention went to the UAG price in Euros.

"We just made 1.4 billion ED on our short trade!" shouted Alain.

"We'll make ten times that in government contracts and business deals," the old man estimated.

Congratulations from Council members popped up on the screen. Apparently, all the fuss over taking out Steinberg was in the past. Time and money would heal all wounds. Now they could plan the takeover of larger countries.

*****

Nick stumbled over a rock, as he tried to keep up with Sandi and Susie in the Jamaican darkness. They cautiously approached the rickety old dock that was to be their rendezvous point. There was a soft bird-like whistle. Susie made a weak attempt to answer, but she was a lousy whistler. Two men emerged from the shadows.

"Sandi, Nick, this is Barboza," Vitale whispered. "Susie already knows him."

They felt their way to the thirty-two-foot Sea Ray. After casting off the lines, they pushed out into the placid water.

"Susie, I'm sorry I didn't catch onto this damn thing sooner," Barboza said.

"No problem," Susie reassured him. "You were the first one to let me know that the intelligence agencies were going into business for themselves. A lot of others were in a better position to know, but didn't tell me."

"Well, my team has it all set up to take these bastards down!" he promised.

Their course was set for Grand Cayman. The plan was to swim ashore on the Cobalt Coast. Scuba divers were common there, so they would blend in.

"Can you swim?" Barboza asked Nick.

"Yes, but I've never dived."

"Don't worry," Barboza assured him, "we'll keep you in the center. Just make sure to keep these thick flippers on and don't touch down with your hands and body. The coral is razor sharp!"

After a short swim, they reached the beach and hid their gear in the scrub behind it. The group set out for a secluded site on the flight path to the airport. Barboza had obtained the tail numbers for Lemond's jets. Barboza's team had set up surveillance cameras outside suspect banks.

Lying concealed in the brush, it was a long hot vigil. Plane after plane flew over them with no results. Suddenly, Barboza sat up to get a better look at the shimmering Gulfstream jet.

"That's it, we've got them," Barboza shouted. "Nick, I hope you're ready to write the biggest story of your career!"

They donned their tourist gear to okay a shuttle to Washington Street and tried to mingle in with the cruise ship crowd. They turned the corner onto a side street and entered a small souvenir shop. Barboza approached the muscular islander behind the counter.

"I ordered a blue salt water crocodile," he said loudly.

The man shrugged and replied, "I don't remember it, but it might be in today's shipment. You're welcome to go in the back and look for it."

Barboza led the team through the parted curtain, around a corner and entered a code into an electronic lock. The heavy metal door opened to reveal a stairway.

The upstairs smelled harshly of mold. In stark contrast, an entire wall, with state-of-the-art monitors displayed images of major international banks. The team stood watching the monitors for two hours.

"There they are!" Sandi shouted.

"Who's the guy on the right?" Susie asked.

"That's the Finance Minister of Jamaica," Barboza said through clenched teeth.

He entered codes on the keyboard below the monitor. Video and data from the bank began to flow simultaneously to Interpol, the *Atlanta Examiner,* and Nick's communicator.

An athletic young man sprinted up the steps of the old hotel in Lyon. He banged on the door of the Master Suite.

"Monsieur Claude, urgent news from Alain in the Cayman Islands!"

Epilogue

The stabbing pain cut through the back of Alain's thigh like a flaming sword as the small dingy trawler crashed through a large wave. The wise old captain held his course steady, ignoring the screams and curses of his celebrity passenger. He had a greater responsibility; navigating through the Caribbean without a GPS or running lights. Of course, he had done it for many years as a smuggler, but new hazards could always pop up and sink the boat of an inattentive captain.

"I'm sorry Monsieur Lemond," the captain said, looking back over his shoulder. "It's better to head into the waves than to take them sideways. There is only one jolt, rather than two!"

Lemond grumbled unintelligibly. The day had started out so well. He had spent a very pleasurable night with a stunningly beautiful Cuban woman that he had met at the hotel. This was not unusual. Women were always attracted to rich and powerful men. He had the bonus of being moderately handsome. He only learned in the morning, that her name was Eliana Suarez and that she was a tourism representative for Cuba. He invited her to spend the day with him, hoping for another incredible adventure in the bedroom. She happily agreed after he promised to introduce her to Cayman financial leaders.

They enjoyed a seafood feast at the Caribe Credit Bank, which featured sea turtle soup. Eliana flirted with the Jamaican Finance Minister, but eventually returned to Alain's side during lunch. Bank employees scrambled to load currency into an armored truck for transport to the Lemond jet. The next stop on the itinerary was to be Monaco. Alain wondered how Eliana would look on his arm as he made his entrance into the Monaco Grand Casino, but decided against it. He had a reputation as a Europhile and he needed to keep it. Great sex wasn't worth losing prestige with the Council. He could always schedule some business trips to Cuba.

The weather was hot and sunny as the elite party broke up and spilled into the street. The laughter stopped suddenly as a heavily armed cadre of men and women attempted to surround them. Alain's security force reacted expertly, shielding him and breaking a path to allow him to escape. They paid with their lives, as withering point-blank gunfire cut them to pieces.

Felix James, the Finance Minister, grabbed Alain's arm, and the two ran down the narrow street toward the docks. Alain's left leg collapsed, causing him to sprawl onto the pavement. Felix practically carried him the last block and onto the boat. Only then did they notice the stream of blood and they realized Alain had been shot. Felix applied a crude field dressing to Alain's leg, laid him on a soft cushion, and then rushed to the bridge to supervise their departure.

Felix returned with a deep scowl on his face. He was a strategic planner, who employed a rigid linear style. Nothing at the London School of Economics had prepared him to manage this situation. His only instinct was to escape to his own turf.

"What did you find out?" Alain demanded.

"Our Intelligence group firmly believes that this was a CIA operation. They can't be one-hundred-percent certain, because they all managed to disappear without a trace!"

Alain looked puzzled as he stared out into the darkness. "How the hell could that happen?" he snapped. "We own the CIA!!"

"It could have been a rogue team, maybe a bank robbery gone bad," Felix speculated. "Don't worry though, the money is secure."

They sat in silent meditation as only the rhythmic waves and the muffled sound of the engine played in the background. Alain bolted upright as a panicked thought raced through his brain. Could this have been planned by someone inside the Council? Could Steinberg's ghost be reaching up from the grave for vengeance? His suspicion immediately focused on Hauptman. He had seemed happy to be rid of Steinberg, but who could know for certain? Was this buyer's remorse, or maybe blind ambition gone off the rails?

The green light on Felix's mobile unit flashed, as the encrypted signal from the satellite awakened it. Felix's eyes widened as he read the text.

"The team was led by the former U. S. Director of Intelligence," he announced.

Alain kicked the bulkhead and immediately regretted it when a stabbing pain shot through his leg. "That bitch!" he screamed. "This was just workplace violence, because I had her fired!"

Felix dropped the other piece of bad news. "The Cuban girl was the mole on the inside," he said glumly.

Alain mentally crossed out any trips to Cuba.

As the boat began steadily to erode the distance to Kingston, the two men decided to brainstorm their strategy.

"The cash is stored in a secret warehouse," Felix mused. "We can report it as a bank robbery, and then move it out of the country on one of our ships."

Alain was stunned. It was a diabolically brilliant plan! They could collect from the insurance company and then filter the cash through their ghost networks. As a bonus, the hunters would become the hunted. Every law enforcement agency in the world would be looking for that rogue CIA team.

The green light on the mobile caught their attention. Once again Felix scrolled through the copious information, but only delivered the highlights.

"Our ships have us in sight and we're under their umbrella of protection," he said flatly. "We'll get your wound treated and then your grandfather will be joining us for breakfast!"

*****

Susie was exhausted and frustrated as they lay in the sand, on an island that had no name. After dropping off the members of Barboza's team in Granada, they raced full speed for over three hours and scuttled the boat a quarter mile off shore. Swimming to the beach, while dragging the equipment, had spent all of their stamina.

"I can't believe we missed that slippery bastard," she complained.

"Not entirely true," Sandi corrected her. "I did hit him! Too bad I miscalculated the trajectory drop at that distance."

"Well, at least you're even," Barboza said with a sardonic smile. "His people shot you, and you got him!"

"Not really," Sandi disagreed, "he still owes me for Nick!"

"Where the hell are we anyway?" Susie snapped.

Barboza took a long moment before responding. He had kept this secret from Washington for four years.

"This island is only about twenty-five years old. It was too small for anyone to notice, especially since it's outside the paths of our tracking satellites. We discovered it during the time the Agency was fragmenting into groups that had their own agendas. We called it 'our place,' and we never told anyone."

Nick was concerned. "How are we supposed to survive here?"

Barboza broke into a broad smile, "Because, when we set it up as 'our place,' we set it up as a doomsday survival location. There's a small inland fresh-water lake, and a secure bunker next to it. We can survive here for a few decades, but I'm hoping that won't be necessary!"

They all struggled to their feet and set out to see their new home. Barboza led them in circles around a small hill.

"You'll have to be patient with me," he explained, "we designed the door to blend into the terrain."

After a brief search, he finally located a twelve-by-twelve-foot door and entered an electronic code into the adjacent panel. It opened to reveal an LCD screen. Barboza pressed his little finger on it, while staring at the dot in the center. The sophisticated scanners recognized him, and the massive door slid open.

Nick whistled softly. "That's some garage door," he remarked reverently, "what's it made from?"

"It's a composite that's undetectable by radar or laser," Barboza said. "It can also withstand an artillery shell."

The narrated tour of the huge facility continued.

"Are you planning to provision an army here?" Sandi asked. She was impressed with all the high tech weaponry.

"I have two-hundred-eighty-seven people on my team," Barboza replied. "This site can house one-hundred-twenty, so obviously, we have a second facility!"

"Is that what I think it is?" Susie asked, staring at an elaborate control panel.

"Yes," he replied. "It's a SADIE air defense system! We got it from the Israelis. It cost us a ton of money!"

"How come you never told me any of this?" Susie observed sadly.

"Susie, you know my team and I are totally loyal to you," he said softly. "Washington was a crazy town, and we didn't have a clue what was happening. We couldn't have any leaks."

"Apparently, neither did I," she said, "and I lived and worked there!"

They picked out their living areas carefully, since they had no idea how long they would be staying. Sandi and Nick lashed together two single beds. The planners of this facility evidently hadn't thought about couples. They talked about where they could go to be intimate and, as always, Sandi was pragmatic.

"Let's scout the place out," she suggested. "I don't want to make love on top of a missile silo!"

"There's always the water," he suggested.

"You're not afraid of catching crabs?" she asked.

They both laughed hysterically at the pun.

A loud whistle called them back to the common area.

"Bad news," Barboza announced. "We're big time bank robbers and terrorists it seems. The Navy is starting a grid search!"

"That's great!" joked Vitale, "I can send my grandchildren to college. How much did we get?"

"A little under $2 billion," Barboza said, laughing.

The jokes didn't last long, as they realized that the Navy would be pressured to search the Caribbean and beyond thoroughly. Barboza assured them that the search wouldn't last very long.

"No one knows about my network. They've only identified the five of us. My compadres will find out what that slippery bastard did with the money, then everyone will be gunning for him!"

Vitale was uneasy. "What about the Cuban girl, the one that was on the inside?" he inquired.

"She is the safest of all," Barboza assured him. "They call her 'La Chameleona.' She and her plastic surgeon change her appearance after each assignment. I don't even know her real name!"

*****

Weeks dragged by, but no information about the money was forthcoming. Living in a tropical paradise was a small comfort. Nick kept busy by writing stories that they snuck out to Diogenes, who published them in the *Examiner.*

Barboza's creative network kept tabs on the Navy's search efforts and discovered they were getting too close.

One morning, a seaplane circled the island, and then landed on the inland lake. The pilot emerged from the plane, inflated a large rubber raft, and paddled to shore. He and Barboza embraced for two or three minutes. Barboza introduced him to the group as Tuli, his right-hand man.

They were a strange combination. Tuli was a descendant of the Inca tribe, while Barboza had strong Portuguese bloodlines. In centuries past, they would have been mortal enemies, but, in this century, they were best friends. "Okay," Barboza thundered, "pack up your gear. Tuli's going to give us a ride to our new home!"

After several hours of flight and a long hot trek through the jungle, they arrived at a clearing, and saw several large bunkers. They appeared to be made of the same material as the one in the island.

"Where are we now?" Nick asked.

Barboza laughed, "The borders around here aren't too clear. Let's just say we're in the middle of the

Amazon rain-forest. The standard of living is a little higher than on the island."

Sandi looked around at the dense jungle. "How are the snakes?" she asked.

"If you cook them right, they really don't taste too bad!" Barboza joked, chuckling.

They all settled in and prayed for a short stay.